COURTING DANIEL'S DAUGHTER

DANIEL'S DAUGHTERS
BOOK ONE

MINDY STEELE

ISBN 979-8-9924497-1-6 (paperback); 979-8-9924497-0-9 (ebook)

Jesse Plank promised to keep a secret. A secret that drove him away from his home eight years ago. But when an old friend calls to share his father has been injured, Jesse must return to help provide for his family. Finding Catherine still the beauty he remembered might convince him to stay.

Catherine Raber has overcome much. Becoming Amish wasn't the same as being born Amish. Thankfully, her terrible school years are behind her and life is looking up. That was until the last person she ever wanted to see again arrived in Miller's Creek. Worse, her father just gave him a job.

Can the truth reveal a different man in Catherine's eyes? Can she accept that she too is flawed?

My faithful readers. May you always find hope and love within my pages.

Glossary

ach : oh

aenti: aunt

bish du base ob mee- Asking someone if they are mad at you

boppli/bopplin: baby, babies

bruder: bother

bu/buwe: boy, boys

daed: dad

danke: thank you

dochter: daughter

dokter: doctor

EE kaw sell nit glauba: I cannot believe that.

Englisch/Englischer: a non-Amish person

Es ish ke fershtant: Used often when speaking to a child that something is not sensible.

fraa: wife

freinden: friend

faul: lazy

goot: good

Gott: God

huck yerst ahna: just sit down

hund: hound or dog

Jah: yes

kaffi: coffee

kapp: prayer covering

kichlin: cookies

kinner: children

komm ena: come in

maed/maedel: girl, young woman

mamm/mammi: mom, grandmother

mariye: morning

nacht: night

nee: no
nix: nothing
onkel: uncle
schwester: sister
sell ist goot: that is good
schee: pretty
sohn: son
vunderbar- wonderful

CHAPTER 1

*J*esse Plank stood in the cold, pouring down Kentucky rain as the car sped out of the driveway. Lifting the collar of his weather-worn coat, he turned to the small, humble house he once called home. A lamp flickered in the window across the way, winking him a welcome. It was the same visual that bid him farewell eight years ago.

Taking in a breath, he released it slowly. No sense in letting insecurities eat at him now. When you burned bridges and didn't rebuild them, what did you expect? He'd have no welcome home supper or teary-eyed mother pulling him into a hug. No, Jesse wouldn't get any of that. Not leaving as he had.

When Paul Eicher, Jesse's oldest childhood friend, called about what had happened, Jesse didn't hesitate hitching a ride from Wisconsin to Kentucky, home. It gave him nine hours to prepare for this reunion of sorts. At least *Daed* hadn't been killed when a truck slammed into his buggy, but with both arms broken, Eli Plank couldn't work. Jesse was their only child. Now their livelihood would fall on Jesse's shoulders.

Paul had no idea what he was asking when he called for

Jesse to return home. But maybe he did. Best friends could do that. *The past is the past,* Jesse mentally schooled himself. He had moved past it well enough. Time could do that, help a man forget.

It also turned cabbage to kraut, apples into vinegar.

Telling the truth about that night, that he wasn't the driver behind the wheel of a wrecked sheriff's car, meant Jesse had to reveal exactly where he was. He couldn't do that. He'd not break that promise. No one would have believed him anyhow after Irvin Miller started the rumor mill going.

Rain continued to pellet Jesse's face as he stared at the house, trying to work up some of that gumption that had carried him along this far. He left Miller's Creek at sixteen, full of arrogance and bitterness, but was returning a man who had learned to control both. The world was good at serving up lessons a man needed to grow. His father would see that. If Eli Plank knew what obstacles God had put Jesse through, the long cold nights and harrowing days that made him appreciate life and things like character, he would see it. *Mamm* would be happy to know he'd held firm to his faith, even in a world that worked hard to shed a man of it.

Convinced forgiveness awaited him, Jesse gripped the black duffle with his few precious belongings and narrowed the distance between yesterday and today. His denim jeans lapped up rain hungrily.

"People change," he reminded himself. Hopefully that included fathers. Eight years of wandering certainly put Jesse through changes. But deep in the core of his own making, Jesse still longed for steady roots, a family that had all its working parts. He hadn't found that out there. Hopefully it was here, where he always wanted it to be. This *was* home and Jesse still wanted the one thing he hadn't found. The one thing wandering hadn't provided.

A family.

And that started here, or ended here, depending on his next move. He knocked on his parent's front door.

THE NEXT MORNING, Jesse slid into the buggy seat next to Paul as sunlight spilled over Sugar Hill. "Thanks for letting me stay at your place last night." Cool misty air nipped at his cheeks. Winter was dying, and he, for one, was glad to see it go.

"I can't believe Eli is so stubborn. Figured Sara, your own *mamm*, would have at least let you sleep in the barn." Paul was a mountain of a man next to Jesse. His once white hair had crusted over with earthier tones and reached to his neckline. Paul had been Jesse's only correspondence over the last eight years. A postcard of his current job in whatever community he dropped into, or a once-a-month letter there, containing any funds Jesse could spare for his parents.

"And go against *Daed*'s orders," Jesse said mockingly. Some things didn't change no matter how much time passed. "I'm not even baptized, and they shun me like a heathen."

Mamm would never go against anything Eli Plank spoke into command. That ghostly look on her face when she opened the door last night still barbed him. Part shock, part relieved. Sara Plank looked nothing like the mother Jesse remembered, but she didn't look disappointed. No, not that. She was thinner, paler, her flesh more ashen than ivory. Time had not been kind to her.

Paul veered the horse down the next lane and soon three open buggies fell in line behind them, forming a parade of clip-clop cadence. Others too were heading to the bi-weekly church service. Jesse suspected few would recognize him. A man did a lot of changing in eight years.

"Don't. Don't pity me." Jesse shifted noting the sorrowful scowl on Paul's face. "It's just a raw spot to know your *daed* disowns you."

"He is set in his ways more than most." Paul agreed.

Eli Plank was a loud and boisterous man. He made outlandish jokes in public, but in the privacy of his home, he was someone else entirely. That voice, the barking one, Jesse hadn't forgotten it in his absence. It had followed him from Michigan to Montana, and it was there last night in bucket-dumping rain when he ordered his son to leave.

SHOVING LAST NIGHT ASIDE, Jesse focused on his surroundings. The roads still bent slightly here, and the hills still shadowed an eastern sunrise. He'd seen his share of mountains, each a majestic wonder, but they didn't compare to the woods plundered with the deer trails he still knew by heart. The lingering creek that ran from one end of the community to the other pulled his attention. Jesse stepped back to a time when life was simple, and a man had solid ground beneath his feet.

Paul turned down another lane, and recognition hit. Soon the mill where his father worked came into view.

The mill.

"Wait, where is the gathering today?" With familiarity, came apprehension.

"You should know where we are," Paul smirked in that same cocky way he used to do when he won at basketball or caught the most fish. "It hasn't been that long."

Jesse did know, and when the house came into view just over the rise, shadowed under a three-story red barn, his pulse accelerated. Jesse had few regrets, but this one haunted him no matter how far he traveled. He had failed to tell the one person who meant the most to him how he truly felt before leaving Miller's Creek, and Paul had brought him straight to her door.

"I wish you would have worn some of my clothes. You're going to stick out in jeans and that ugly shirt." Paul brought the buggy to a halt in front of Daniel Raber's barn. Jesse gave his clothes a quick glance over. Little he could do about that now.

"You are a foot taller. Wearing *your* clothes would make me stick out." Jesse bounced out of the buggy, and all eyes were on him. He was practiced in being the new face in a community, but unease soured his stomach. This had been the community of his upbringing. The people he knew all his life. Most wouldn't recognize him. Not after so many years. They'd think him a newcomer, or an *Englischer* seeking out the good life.

"It wonders me why you didn't tell me last night who the hosting family was." Jesse cocked a brow.

"Why use a feather when a hammer will do?" Paul chuckled as he unharnessed his horse and led him to pasture. Paul was a man of few words, but what words he did speak, made an impact and it was as annoying as it was when they were *kinner*.

"Besides, if you're serious about joining the church and settling down, might as well toss you into the deep end while you're fresh. I hear swimming works better that way."

That's exactly what Paul had done. Jesse should have never revealed his hope for sticking around. His gaze traveled to a

5

field full of more than thirty goats. His eyes narrowed curiously. "I could always outswim you and Aiden both. Are those... goats?" Jesse motioned towards the back field. The Daniel Raber he remembered wielded an ax and rolled logs onto skids for sawing like they were mere twigs. Now the man was a goat farmer?

"The *schwestern* make good money with them. M.J. sold one last year for over twelve hundred dollars."

Jesse knew a good stud or strong blooded bull was worth more than its weight, but a pesky goat?

"She milks them for the family's cheese business."

"Cheese business?"

"*Jah*, Rosemary helps make cheese, and she raises bees for honey. M.J. sells both at the marketplace in town. You have missed quite a bit."

Jesse didn't need Paul reminding him. Closing his eyes he breathed in the fresh scent of hay and horses, of damp earth and spring. *God, I missed this.* Opening his eyes, Jesse began his search. In all his travels there was at least one thing Jesse Plank had never forgotten about Miller's Creek, and that was a set of china blue eyes and a laugh that could bring a man to attention.

Daniel Raber had three daughters. M.J., the youngest, was all smiles and adventures. Rosemary, the middle daughter, was the spitting image of her *daed*. A delicate, shy girl who made you fear she would break if you looked at her the wrong way. Jesse had been careful not to tease that one. Unlike Catherine, no fire lit up in her eyes that tempted a boy to keep poking.

Catherine. Even now her name rested sweet on his tongue. Jesse had teased her for a time when teasing was innocent and earned you a few laughs. By the time she reached thirteen, he was terrified of her. But he outgrew that fear the week of his sixteenth birthday when the little girl who liked to argue with him became the young woman who made his heart race faster than an eight horse team behind the plow.

"Hiya, old friend," Aiden Shetler marched their way. "I thought you were up in Michigan working on a cranberry bog."

Jesse smiled, taking in the boy he remembered. They had the same build, but Aiden's light hair and blue eyes made him more day to Jesse's dark night. "It's cold, wet work. Worse than working cattle in Montana in January. I don't know how my cousin James stands it year after year." Jesse didn't miss it, but was grateful for the experience. He loved moving from one place to another, no attachments, nothing holding him down, no one to disappoint for a time. Now he wanted something more.

"You're blessed." Aiden shrugged. "Seeing all of that. Not doing the same thing everyday. Life here is boring."

"Not everyone wants to worry where to lay their head at night," Paul put in, always the reasonable one.

"Exactly," Jesse seconded. "Out there may look nice, but nice doesn't keep a man warm and fed." Aiden didn't know just how blessed he was, living a normal life.

"Speaking of nice, there's my little milk maiden now," Aiden interrupted, his gaze focused solely on the house. Rows of yellow daffodils and colorful tulips skirted the front walkway. Aiden threw up a hand just as a pretty blonde threw up hers and floated a beaming smile their way.

"Who's that?" Jesse didn't recognize her, but that smile did seem familiar.

"That, my friend, is Martha Jane Raber, all grown up." Paul dropped an arm on Jesse's shoulders. Jesse could see it now. The small, rounded face dominated by big brown eyes that still held joy and jokes equally. Paul nodded just behind her. "And that would be..."

Paul didn't need to finish. Jesse's eyes worked just as good as his memory. There she was, leaned over tying the shoes for two little boys about school age. Jesse's heart ceased all functions and then slapped him with a punch. No, no one needed to point her out. Jesse would know that heart shaped face anywhere.

Had she married? Were those her *kinner*? "Who's the *kinner*?"

"That would be Henry and Bryan, Daniel's two *sohns*," Paul replied. "Remember when I wrote to you about the bishop's horses getting out, and it took everyone two days to round them up?" Paul pointed. "Well, that was their doing. They are a pair for sure and certain." Paul laughed, but Jesse's unflinching attention was set straight on Catherine as a shaft of sunlight poured over her. God's exclamation point, he supposed.

Catherine hadn't noticed him yet, and Jesse quickly contemplated his next move. Why was this first encounter making him so nervous? He had wrangled steers with more power and climbed higher altitudes than her suggested five-foot few inches pronounced. Still his palms were growing slick at the sight of her. She probably wouldn't even recognize him, to tell the truth. Part of him hoped she didn't until he was ready, and right now, he clearly wasn't.

She laughed as the boys ran off and then suddenly, Catherine bristled. Those senses were just as keen as they had been at fifteen when she caught him staring at her during the community picnic. She always caught him. When she turned his way, tilting her head, his heart began a new beat.

CHAPTER 2

*C*atherine Raber felt today was the day. The day Irvin Miller would finally notice her. Overnight April rains left a chill in the two-story house that felt much like winter wanted to linger. Catherine fetched her sweater from the bedpost, slipping it on just as footsteps ran down the hallway toward the attic. With a roll of her eyes, she hurried after the little thieves stealing precious time, again. There was much to do yet, but right now her vexing duty included urging the two brown eyed tricksters out of playing games and readying for Sunday gathering.

"Oh where is Henry? Oh where is Bryan?" she growled playfully as both boys giggled from behind the door. Catherine put aside the late hour and tried being purposely more fun. Perhaps she was too serious, as M.J. accused her of being. Then again, her youngest sister had the ability to turn slug racing into exciting.

"Come out, come out wherever you are." More giggles. Catherine sprang forward with arms reaching, "Gotcha!"

"Oh Cat, you find us too fast. I don't like it," Henry pouted with one of his signature pouts. Bryan, of course, mocked his stance and puckered both lips accordingly, always the follower that one. Catherine smiled at their matching features and Sunday best. Adorable, that's what they were.

"It's because she is the best seeker," Rosemary said entering the room with two small coats in hand. "I never could hide from her, ever," Rosemary said with a soft smile. "Now come on with you. I could use some help in the barn before everyone starts arriving." Rosemary helped the boys into their coats, ignoring their grumbling complaints. Her ability to dismiss protests was why she was considered the sweetest sister.

"Perhaps today will be the day," Rosemary whispered before reaching the side door and slipping on her own coat.

"Perhaps it will be," Catherine hoped. It was hard to keep a secret in a full house. Perhaps Catherine hadn't been so quiet in vying for Irvin's attention after all, but he was speaking to her more and more at each gathering recently. Surely he had an interest.

Rosemary ushered the *buwe* outside where they hopped between mud puddles before vanishing into the barn. Catherine couldn't keep from smiling. Oh, how she longed for *kinner* of her own someday.

"What can I do?" Catherine asked *Mamm* as she stepped into the kitchen. Catherine mirrored her in many ways, but most noticeably their blue eyes. All her siblings had brown eyes, making this one thing she and her mother shared alone.

"Put the beans and the broccoli casserole in the oven to stay warm, please. Your *daed* sliced all the ham last night." Catherine got in step, knowing her way around a kitchen as much as she did around a sawmill. It was important for a *maedel* to learn as much as she could. At least Catherine believed it so.

"I hope *Daed* finds a new sawyer to fill in for Eli soon," Catherine said, sliding the casseroles into the oven. Since Eli Plank's buggy accident last week, her father had been shorthanded at the mill and lumber orders were backing up as spring was now here.

"It's not easy to find someone who knows how to do such work," *Mamm* replied while untying her chore apron.

"Perhaps we can pray about it. We need a sawyer and sunshine." *And for Irvin Miller to finally take notice of me*, Catherine silently added.

"It's a new day, and anything can happen," her mother added with her typical whimsical tone. With the sound of buggies coming up the family drive, Catherine hoped she was right.

Within an hour folks began gravitating toward the barn. When she spotted Bryan and Henry fooling around the manure pit, she quickly made her way towards them before *Daed* noticed. It took half a day's work to keep those two from trouble.

"Time to head to the barn before Daed sees you," she warned.

"But..." Henry began, but a sharp glance helped him think better of it.

"Step over here," Catherine said in a frustrated breath. "Your shoes aren't even tied!" She knew two little *bruders* who desperately needed to learn to tie their own shoes before another trip to the hospital happened. "How many times must I remind you not to run with your shoes untied?" Catherine finished pulling the knot on Bryan's shoes and gave both boys a hardened look.

"One more time I guess," Bryan answered with an innocent shrug. Catherine refrained from smiling. That would only encourage them. *The little smarty*. She rose back to her feet and watched the two scurry off inside. Suddenly, an abrupt awareness came over her, lifting the hairs on her neck and arms. The way one did when the conscious sent a forewarning.

Turning, Catherine's eyes locked with a set of brown eyes across the yard, and her pulse spiked immediately.

He was a stranger for sure and certain. Catherine would have remembered seeing him before. He looked completely at ease and not as if standing out, which he was in denim pants and a shirt. She'd heard of seekers, those tempted to experience the world through Amish faith and simplicity, but this was the first time one had visited their district before. He had dark hair and eyes and shoulders that looked capable of carrying their fair share. He felt oddly familiar.

Taking a long inhale, her eyes traveled back to his face. When his lips hiked into a grin, Catherine knew he was acknowledging her. It was only right to smile back. Then her common sense took over, and she dropped her gaze quickly. No respectful Amish *maedel* stared this way. She glanced about; thankfully no one witnessed the encounter. Tongues would be wagging for sure and for certain at her googly-eyeing a handsome *Englischer*. What if Irvin thought her an attention seeker like Mollie Lapp or Mary Beiler? It had only been a week since he complimented her new teal dress. Of course, that wasn't flirtation or a promise, but he noticed.

Catherine hurried into the barn, ignoring the mysterious newcomer, but their awkward encounter, the way he smiled at her, couldn't be ignored. Looks could be powerful things. They could threaten or show interest without mumbling a word. His had her nerves tripping. If she caught him staring again, she would offer a sharp look. That's what she would do. She had no interest in a man who straddled fences in his faith.

After the three-hour service, Catherine quickly flowed in line with the other women to ready the fellowship meal. The *Englisch* stranger had become all the whispers. Half the *maedels* on Catherine's bench alone had spent the entire church service staring his way instead of listening to the minister's sermon. If they had been listening, they would have learned a thing or two about distractions. A good Amish *maedel* didn't get distracted by the worldly, and he most certainly was worldly from the way he dressed.

"That man is staring at you again," Ivy Troyer whispered as Catherine went to retrieve a pitcher of freshly made sweet tea from the kitchen.

"He is a bold one, that's for sure." She feigned a lack of interest despite feeling flattered to have earned someone's attention. "We should grab more *kichlin* too. I noticed the plate is empty." Ivy lifted a plate of assorted cookies.

"*Jah*, those Graber *buwe* have been swiping them every time Hazel Miller turns her head." The friends laughed, knowing full well how Silas Graber's youngest was most likely working alone.

Slipping out the kitchen side door, Irvin called out to her, bringing both women to a halt. Catherine had hoped that he would.

Ivy shot her a smile. "I'll just take the tea, and you take the *kichlin,*" Ivy winked. "Perhaps today is the day." Ivy took the pitcher of tea and offered Catherine the plate of cookies.

Perhaps today was the day. The day God's plan for her would reveal itself. She tried to walk as normal as possible. If the stranger with brown eyes had not already rattled her, it wouldn't have been so difficult to do.

"Hiya." Irvin welcomed. Not quite six foot, but his light brown hair and soft blue eyes always made her look twice. And *Daed* liked him, she reminded herself. Well, *Daed* never said an ill thing against him, so that was pretty much the same. She could never consider a man *Daed* didn't approve of because no man would compare to Daniel Raber in his daughter's eyes. His love for each of them was unequivocal. He proved it when he gave them shelter, coddled their fears, and dried their tears. And he proved it when he loved their mother fully and unconditionally. Catherine could only hope that one day she could be so fortunate.

"I made *kichlin*, if you want to sneak a few." She smiled coyly, remembering all too well how he scoffed at her cookies the last time she brought them to a gathering. She had been practicing her flirting. Rosemary thought it ridiculous, and M.J. was simply a natural at it. Catherine was not letting her baby sister marry before her.

"I will never refuse sweets." Irvin took two and shot her a wink, causing her insides to quiver. She would not show jitters, she schooled herself. Did all *maedels* get this nervous?

"I wanted to ask to drive you home today, but…" He glanced about the yard. Catherine laughed. Hosting church at your own home didn't make for a long ride. Irvin neared, placing a large hand on her elbow. She found the contact just as nerve rattling as strangers looking at her. Lifting her chin, she collected herself. Surely all *maedels* experienced this. The first touches, the confusing thoughts. Her flirting skills were working just fine apparently. She had in fact caught Irvin Miller's attention.

Catherine wanted marriage like all *maedels* of her age, and this was part of the process. But was she really ready for courting and flirting, and, Lord be it, kissing? Catherine took a step back.

"A walk perhaps." She had no idea where that came from. *Daed likes him*, she reminded herself again. And there was no way she was going to court one of the pesky Lewis brothers. Known for their lingering Rumspringa and unhealthy cigarette habits, she could smell the strong effects on Felty Lewis at six feet away. Catherine didn't know why Irvin saddled himself to the two so often. He joined the church early on, before his eighteenth birthday. Helped others and never had a bad word said against him. He was a worthy match.

"Me and a few others are going to the lake; thought you

might like to join," Mollie Lapp strolled up, speaking directly to Irvin. Catherine pretended not to be offended. Barely seventeen and already batting eyelashes. It was shameful.

"Well, I'm sure Felty and Sam here would love to. I'm…" he turned to Catherine, "thinking a walk on this *schee* day is in order." Catherine's spirits lifted immediately. Mollie was very pretty and already receiving attention from others. Catherine was just plain. Her hips were straight, her chin too pointy, and she would never fill a dress like Mollie.

"What's he doing here?" Irvin's face dipped into a scowl. Turning, she noted her *daed* and the bishop chatting with the *Englischer*. He laughed at something that was said. He had a nice smile, all pearly and wide and drawing. He was far too handsome for words. She jerked from gawking when a hand touched her elbow again.

"Sorry, Catherine," he stuttered. "I forgot I have somewhere to be, but Monday we will have supper with my family, and we'll take that walk." Mouth agape and full plate of cookies in hand, Catherine watched Irvin march away abruptly. Not exactly how she envisioned this first successful encounter. Catherine turned back to the newcomer who had caused Irvin to change his mind. When that dark gaze collided with hers this time, he wasn't smiling.

CHAPTER 3

*C*atherine worked the strings of her apron front as she stepped into the kitchen. In the dim lamp light, she could make out the shadows of her parents with their heads together, whispering in soft tones. She smothered a giggle behind her hand and quickly lowered her gaze. They were ridiculously happy and hopelessly in love, even at their age.

Mamm deserved a forever love, and *Daed* never slacked giving it to her. Catherine wanted that. A marriage that withstood the ins and outs of raising a family and the resilience to deal with the unexpected that always came along. She wanted a man who, in one simple look, made her knees go wobbly and her smile widen…for their rest of their lives.

"I agree. I'm just surprised, but then again, you are the sweetest man I know," her mother murmured and kissed *Daed's* cheek. "Does he know enough to run the saw?"

"You found a sawyer?" From the shadows, Catherine squealed in delight. "*Sell ist goot.*" Her parents passed a quick look to each other before turning to face her.

"I hired a man, not sure I'd call him good," *Daed* said,

unimpressed before noticing Catherine's new dress. "You look mighty nice for a dirty old mill today." Daniel gathered two fatherly brows as he studied the dark blue of freshly sewn material.

"I have plans for after work today. I won't have time to run home and change since my employer rarely lets me leave early," Catherine replied playfully. "*Mamm* helped me finish it. Isn't it just the richest shade of blue?" She spun, hoping to distract him from the parade of questions resting on his frown.

"And what would this something be?" Catherine stopped spinning. She should have known.

"I'm having supper at the Miller's house." Catherine lifted her chin, something she always did when she wanted him to know she really wanted something.

"You're a *youngie*." His eyes narrowed.

"I'm twenty-four." Far from being a teenager. Catherine retrieved a coffee cup from a cabinet left of the sink.

"He's not my first choice," Daniel continued, scratching for excuses. It didn't work on her as it did M.J.

"Irvin has been working at his *daed*'s welding shop for four years." She poured herself a cup of *kaffi*. The pot was light, meaning her parents had already drunk their one cup. Always, just one cup.

"Does that mean you have a list? Perhaps I should look at it before accepting invitations next time." His frown didn't waver, indicating he wasn't content in her choice. Part of that disturbed Catherine terribly. The other part of it simply made her grin. He was such a loving *daed*. Most Amish fathers welcomed their children finding matches, the perfect partner to marry, start a family of their own, and continue as assigned from God. *Daed* held on. He was good at holding on and clearly in no hurry to marry off his *kinner*.

"Not a trade I would stake a future on," Daniel muttered

gruffly, but Catherine knew Irvin held all the qualities her father would deem perfect husband material, once he wrapped his head around his daughter not being a *youngie* any more. "And the list is very, very short." He displayed a thumb and finger to demonstrate just how short.

"Oh, Daniel," *Mamm* scoffed playfully, giving his arm a pat. He groaned again.

"Did I mention I'm twenty-four? I know you approve of him more than those Lewis boys." Catherine pointed him a look before his lips lifted ever so slightly into a smirk. "I guess I could take Margret Sayer's *bruder* up on his offer to court me?" Catherine sipped at her coffee to mask the grin on her face. Margret Sayer had done everything she could to sway *Daed's* heart in her favor before he met her mother. Just the mention of her name always had tension cording in his neck.

"Irvin might be the better of the lot, but I still don't like it. Best you wait on a better one."

"Would you like any man who might want to court one of your daughters?" Catherine knew the answer, and her father didn't reply. He didn't need to. "And that's why you are the best *daed* in the world." She kissed his cheek. "I'm going to help ready the boys for school. See you at the mill in an hour... boss." She bounced off giddily. She was having supper with a man, a possible interest, and dad had finally found a sawyer. Life was looking up. Everything was just as it should be.

An hour later, Catherine slipped her shawl around her shoulders, carefully secured her black bonnet over her *kapp*, and headed towards the mill. Cold, damp morning air filled her lungs while dewy grass licked at her shoes.

The lumber mill rested just over the rise. She loved to walk the worn path and could navigate it even in the dark for all the trips she made running over it in the years. Since her *daed* took her to work with him on that first day, at the age of nine, her sole purpose in life was helping his livelihood to grow. And grow it had. Not only did they saw and sell rough lumber, but mulching had become an extra profit, as well as selling scraps for firewood. Nothing was wasted.

Topping the hill, the sunrise burst into view, blinding her momentarily. Catherine raised a hand and watched her footing as she made a slow descent. In the mill lot, she noticed men had gathered. It was a familiar morning scene, only today there would be a new face among those employed. She smiled at the figures below, her heart full of thanks that God sent help at their time of need, and she couldn't wait to thank the man herself. Perhaps she could bake him a pie or one of her special berry cobblers as a thank you. Everyone liked cobbler.

Daed's tall sturdy silhouette centered the men. To his right, Vernon Schwartz, who had worked at the mill since the start. Paul and Aiden had been working here for almost three years now, though Catherine suspected Aiden only worked here to get closer eyes on M.J. These men had become family, and she cared for them each deeply.

She noted the stranger among them, holding a chainsaw as *Daed* directed him what to do. Catherine hoped he had smarts. Dangers weren't exempt here. Any number of mishaps could lead to misfortune. Broken saw blades, rolling logs, and chainsaws not handled properly were top concerns. Thankfully no one had ever been injured before, but *Daed* was very strict about safety. Still, it never hurt to offer up a quick prayer that things remained that way.

Drawing closer, Catherine collected the stranger's pronounced height. Not like Paul who was freakishly tall for any man, but compared to *Daed* and Aiden, a lofty sort. At least six foot, he was. He yanked on the chainsaw and immediately the familiar buzz came to life. At least he knew how to use one of those; she relaxed. She didn't recognize him as a face from their district at this angle, but wasn't about to disturb the men while working.

Strolling past, Paul caught sight of her out of the corner of his eye and floated Catherine a good morning nod. It was customary of Paul. A gentle giant, *Mamm* called him. Catherine had known Paul for so long she thought of him as a brother and one that listened a whole lot better than the two she was given.

Stepping onto the office porch, Catherine took one last glance over her shoulder. The saw ate through the end of a chestnut log effortlessly under the stranger's hand. Beneath tattered blue trousers, his frame suggested a natural masculinity. He had dark, short cropped hair under his straw hat. She didn't see his face, but the outline of a clean jaw indicated he wasn't a married man.

A sudden rush of warmth skidded over her. She wasn't the type who gawked, and here for two days in a row she had been doing just that at mere strangers. Clearly M.J.'s constant yammering of romance was to blame.

Catherine quickly slipped into the office and smiled, though she hadn't a clue as to why. She was having supper with Irvin and his family tonight. The *Englischer* and the faceless man with strong arms shouldn't be a thought, so she shoved them away. In her home away from home, Catherine began her work

Jesse woke to Paul shaking him. "*Komm*, the bishop and Daniel are here to speak to you," Paul said in a rusty morning voice as he slipped his suspenders over his shoulders.

Jesse grumbled, yanking on his worn out Amish clothes, thin as an onion skin, they did nothing against a breeze, but were still intact. No need to start off on a worse foot than he had already. He had barely slept a wink all night thinking about yesterday. Now fully awake, Jesse couldn't stop thinking again.

Jesse had been half listening as Aiden continued sharing his latest fishing story yesterday when he noticed Catherine carrying a plate of cookies through the front yard. In her royal blue dress, always royal blue, she strolled up to a group. He simply admired her from a distance while working up the courage to speak to her after all these years. Then another familiar face appeared. Leaning too close to Catherine to be considered casual, was Irvin Miller.

He wasn't going to stand there and watch the man who cost him so much talk to Catherine, but before he could walk away, the bishop appeared, along with Catherine's father. And now here they were again. Jesse and Paul quickly shrugged on their boots and went out to meet the elders out on the porch.

Joshua Schwartz was timeless, from his line riddled features to his always distracting pointy beard. *"Mariye,"* Jesse offered both men in a raspy voice. Daniel had no idea how much Jesse had looked up to him growing up. If he did, he wouldn't be frowning so.

"I heard you were staying here with Ben and his family," the bishop quickly put in. Jesse suspected his father had a hand in this early morning visit.

"Eli and Sara must not be pleased that you've returned," Daniel remarked as two roosters decided to take turns announcing daybreak.

"He isn't," Jesse replied honestly and then quickly cleared his throat. He hoped he didn't have to repeat the events of his homecoming publicly. No one wanted their fresh wounds exposed. Thankfully, neither man pressed.

"You plan on staying, or moving on?" The bishop had never been one to linger in getting to a point.

"I'm in no hurry. They need me, even if they don't want to."

"Then we figure you'll be looking for work." The bishop began stroking his beard in long careful strokes.

"Daniel *is* in need of a sawyer," Paul passed the bishop a sly grin. Jesse had a sneaking suspicion the two had already had this conversation. Now Daniel's presence made sense, though Jesse never would have guessed Daniel Raber was willing to offer him a job. Not with his history.

"A worthy sawyer isn't easy to find." Daniel gave Paul a narrowed look before settling his dark eyes on the bishop. *"Onkel,* is this why you asked me to come here with you?"

"I heard you know your way around a mill, *jah?"* Ignoring Daniel, the bishop stopped stroking his beard. Jesse could see Daniel was slowly coming to realize they were being put on the spot.

"Well, you could ask him," Joshua nudged Daniel as he pulled a hard, butterscotch candy from his pocket and began untwisting the wrapper. Jesse stiffened, as did Catherine's father.

Now it made sense. Since Jesse's father had been Daniel's sawyer for years, Daniel was a man short now that his father had been in a buggy accident. Jesse had apprenticed up north, but no way would a man like Daniel trust him at the helm of his livelihood.

"I've learned a few things, *jah*," Jesse said with a slow coolness as he shifted on his left foot.

"The world is mighty good for serving up lessons," the bishop stressed. That was the truth. "And let's not forget there was once a *ferhoodled* young man who came knocking on my door fifteen years ago in need of proving himself, too. The two of you are not so different to me." The bishop split a look between Daniel and Jesse, as if thinking them the same.

That was ridiculous. Jesse was an only child born in a home of little love. Daniel owned a large home, a business, and had a family most men dreamed of. They had nothing in common. Well, almost nothing.

"At what cost," Daniel muttered before running a wide palm down his face. It was clear he was battling between good common sense and Gott's instruction to show kindness to others.

"I suspect you could use a place to lay your head, too?"

"I can manage." Jesse was sleeping in Paul's little *schwesters* bed right now and was sure Little Fran would appreciate having it back, but he wasn't asking for handouts.

"Weather's warming." Daniel eyed the sunrise climbing into the upper valley. "I reckon a cot will do ya. We start at eight, and I don't tolerate *faul* hands."

With that, Daniel Raber turned and headed for the open buggy sitting a few yards away. Bishop Schwartz on the other hand, winked before strolling behind him. Jesse didn't miss the satisfied grin smeared over his face.

Paul slapped Jesse on the back and sidled up beside him as they watched the men drive away. "Seems things are getting more exciting here now that you're home," Paul laughed. "You can't turn work away."

He couldn't. His mother needed cared for, his *daed*, too, despite his unforgiving mindset. "I won't," Jesse replied, still staring after the men as they turned onto the county road.

Daniel was the last person in Miller's Creek Jesse suspected of offering him both work and boarding. It was divine intervention, placing him so close to her. It had disturbed Jesse plenty seeing her speaking to Irvin, but Catherine was a smart woman, at least she had been all the years he knew her. Perhaps they could get to know each other again, the people they were now. Jesse had never been more eager to start a new job.

"Let's get going," Jesse grinned. "Daniel doesn't appreciate tardiness."

Jesse ran the chainsaw all morning, cutting ends off of logs in the lot. Then Daniel assigned him to counting lumber. A boring task, but he learned complaints only gifted you more miserable work.

When he finished counting the last stack of lumber in the first row and secured it with the metal banding required for shipping, Jesse stepped back and glanced up to the sky, ahead and behind a sun that alluded calm. Inhaling, he gorged on the fresh air, and then let it out slowly. In all these years apart from his community, Jesse saw mountains that touched the heavens, and lakes so blue one could spot its inhabitants. He had stood under sunsets that made him feel God's presence, and felt storms that made a man understand how precious every breath was. However, no matter how many trades he learned or faces he encountered, how many valleys he ventured and rivers he crossed, nothing compared to a Kentucky sunrise and the sweet scents of home.

Home.

Daniel had made many improvements. Jesse remembered days of tallying lumber up for his father and shoveling sawdust into massive piles. Adding a mulching machine was a good decision. Jesse hated to see anything go to waste. The world outside of here, he had learned, was wasteful.

He collected the clipboard, slipped the Conway stick used for measuring under an arm, and headed back towards the mill area. He shouldn't have smirked when Daniel asked him if he could even read the meter stick. Jesse could do that and grade lumber too. Though there was little need of it here, sawing rough lumber and stacking it to dry as opposed to the pricey kilns used up north. But the man did soften his scowl a little to know Jesse knew a thing or three about the trade.

"I have those footages you asked for, Daniel." Jesse reached the clipboard out to him. "I think that should fill the Bramel order."

"That was fast. Too fast." Daniel lifted a skeptical brow. Jesse always had a head for numbers, and ignored the jab. It would take some time, leaving as he had, to be trusted by others once more, but it weighed on a man always in a position to earn trust.

"I need to saw and can't go around after you seeing if you can count." Daniel glanced over the clipboard and made a low groaning sound from deep within before shoving it back at Jesse. "Take them into the office. Catherine will double check them, and then get back to stacking with the others. We have a load of cedar coming in this evening from our buyer down south."

By now Catherine would know he was working here and becoming her nearest neighbor too. If living in a barn loft constituted a neighbor, that was. He gripped the clipboard and hesitated. He wasn't ready yet. As bad as he ached to see her, hear her voice after all these years, Jesse simply wasn't ready.

He knew he wasn't that same scraggly boy who wasn't good enough, but that didn't help him right now.

"You waiting for rain or something?" Daniel folded his arms over his chest. It was the same look, the same stance, when Jesse was ten and had teased Catherine about her odd short hair.

"I was a foolish boy back then." Jesse kicked the dirt about him.

"*Jah*, and then some." Daniel put in quick. "Pride is sin. Asking forgiveness smothers it." The two long stretched wrinkles of his forehead sunk deeper. He wasn't prideful and had asked for forgiveness twice since returning. Hopefully three times was a charm.

"*Mei dochter* is a forgiving sort. Now get to it. You want work and to have a roof over your head, then you need to get that out of the way." Daniel pinned him. "Unless you got somewhere else you would rather be."

Jesse's shoulders slumped, purposefully. He knew his place, knew how strong men worked. Daniel was making a sport of watching him squirm. Little did the man know Jesse could lead as easily as he could follow, but Daniel needed him, his skills, and in trade, the man just gave Jesse permission to speak to his *dochter*. Yeah, the world was a good teacher, and sometimes a man had to use what he had.

"You're right," Jesse said before aiming for the mill office.

She was deep in concentration, her full wide mouth unsmiling. In spite of her severe focus, she was beautiful, and completely unaware of his scrutiny. Jesse's imagination had fallen short on just how beautiful time would make her.

Feet planted in place, Jesse studied every serious line and delicate curve of her face from the open doorway. That's when it hit him. The scent of a memory he had held onto for nearly a decade. *Jasmine.* Out west Jasmine grew wild and tall, and could quickly take him back home to Miller's Creek, and her, in just one sniff. Anytime he began to forget, another season would come, another state, and still, the jasmine bloomed. He took in a slow tantalizing inhale as he had decades ago, sitting two rows behind her in school, and let the air fill him like a long lost craving.

Her jaw clenched tightly, something she used to do when thinking hard. It was almost tempting to continue standing there, but Jesse knew Daniel had a perfect view from his stance behind the mill controls of the office, and he had pushed his luck as it was playing the man against himself. If he lingered too long, this long-awaited reunion would be interrupted. Jesse cleared his throat.

"Daniel asked that I bring these in to you."

CHAPTER 4

*T*he stranger's voice was deep and completely unexpected. Catherine released her lip as she jerked her head up from the ledger to meet her father's new hired hand. Startled by his surprising fine looks and casual stance, she quickly got to her feet and brushed her hands down her dress.

"*Danke,*" she reached out to retrieve the clipboard in his hand, but he made no attempt to come further. Instead those dark eyes smiled in odd reverence. He was even more handsome up close, she discovered. A strong jawline, high cheekbones, lips that quirked to one side arrogantly, and he was unapologetically staring.

Catherine swallowed the lump in her throat, trying to gain composure in his gaze. It was only when he tilted his head slightly to the left did something forgotten try niggling its way into her head. *Those eyes. That grin.* Her smile slowly faltered. *The Englischer.* It was the *Englischer* from Sunday who had caught her attention?

"Hello, Catherine Faith."

He knew her name. Catherine had not befriended any

Englischer's since *Mamm* married Daniel, but familiarity couldn't be pushed aside.

"It's been a while," he continued to add.

Upon that, recognition hit, and this time Catherine had no control over the race of adrenalin that surged wildly through her. "Jesse?"

Narrowing her gaze, she could see it. Surely this was a mistake, but rarely did Catherine make mistakes. Staggering backwards, she bumped into the seat of her chair and fell flat on her behind.

"*Jesse Plank*!" His brows lifted, punctuating an amused smile at her high pitched voice. Catherine gritted her teeth on the rest of his name... liar, bully, prankster, and worldly traveler. Oh, she'd heard the rumors of his gallivanting all over the country. Not an Amish bone in his body. The scoundrel. A dangerous man, she mentally reminded herself, with no home, no faith, and no moral compass. She thought him handsome. *Stupid*. Getting back to her feet, as she would not let him see her uncertain, she dug her nails into her palms.

"You are *not* our new help." It wasn't a question. Had *Daed* lost his senses?

"Actually..." He removed his hat, and there was no mistaking it. Those eyes. That grin. Her heart pounded out of control.

"No." She spat out. "You cannot work here!" She had it on good authority that when tempered, her icy blue glare pierced.

"It's nice to see you again too," he said. All those grown, chiseled features began sharpening. He went from smiling to looking almost dangerous and wicked and...beautiful.

No! No! No! It was Jesse. She'd not think him fine looking, but eight years had changed the boy she remembered, a lot. She needed to keep her wits and remembered just who she was truly dealing with.

"I'm supposed to say the same." It was their way to be

welcoming to all, no matter who the *all* was. "Excuse me while I bite my tongue."

"Wow, I saw this going differently," he muttered, rubbing a hand over his neck. "I thought you knew. I mean, you smiled at me at church yesterday, and I figured Daniel told you. I'm really sorry."

"That makes two of us." He watched her with unblinking eyes, the kind that worked like a mirror. She noted the wide eyed expression that was her own and tamped down her sudden shock of seeing him after all this time.

"Daniel needed my help. I accepted." His voice was so much deeper than she remembered.

"I'll tell him to find another." She folded her arms across her chest and shot him a smug look, just as she had when she was a child tattling on him for saying something that hurt her feelings.

"Your protest is a bit late this time." There was the boy she remembered. The one who liked to get her all worked up.

"You...you..." Catherine pointed a finger. "Anyone but YOU!" He moved towards her, only a neatly kept desk between them, and laid the clipboard down before delivering the most handsome smile Catherine had ever encountered. She'd heed well to remember inside that cocky smile was Jesse Plank, the boy who made her growing up years pure misery.

"You look...just as I remembered." He tipped his hat. "See ya at lunch." Without another word, Jesse sauntered out, closing the door behind him.

Catherine's mouth remained open, her face flushed, and she was almost certain she might have drawn blood from her palms. Jesse Plank was the stranger she had smiled at, the man who *Daed* gave work to, and her childhood returned all at once. She placed a hand over her heart and dropped down into her office chair, waiting for the clamor to calm.

Jesse was back in Miller's Creek and closer than ever.

As the breezy work day waned to an end Jesse helped Aiden and Paul load scrap wood in the back of a pick-up. "How'd it go?" Paul asked.

"Not the reunion I had in mind." Jesse tossed another handful into the truck bed. What did he expect after being gone so long? He'd expected Catherine would be breathtaking, stealing the very air in which he needed for survival. God never promised easy. She'd always been pretty, but her girlish looks had morphed into quite the surprise. Too bad she still had a bite sharp enough to pierce into flesh and bone. She wore that same look that melted his twelve-year-old heart.

M.J. had sneaked off to follow them fishing late one night, and Catherine found her before their parents realized she had gone missing. The look on her face, fear, panic, and utter helplessness when she wrapped her sister in her arms, scarred him deeper than any calling life tossed his direction.

Jesse had walked them both home afterward. Catherine scolded her sister, barked about responsibility, and how something could have happened to her and Daniel wouldn't be there to save her.

When they reached their home, Catherine sent M.J. inside and gave Jesse all her remaining wrath. He took it, of course, and watched her protective nature unleash on him. She loved her sister so deeply that she stepped out of her tidy shell of conformity and threatened Jesse with his very life. Promised Aiden and Paul would get an earful as well.

Jesse had fallen in love that night. The night when the most perfect, well-mannered, proper, and beautifully obedient *maedel* in the community became a damaging wind, tearing apart anything in the path of her family's safety. His own mother had never stood up to his *daed* when he inflicted punishment for crimes Jesse hadn't even thought to commit yet, and Catherine was willing to throttle him for M.J. running off.

Jesse huffed, tossing another armload into the truck. Catherine no more wanted to see his face than she wanted a case of chicken pox. *Fool me once*, his head spat to his heart. That's what he got for letting one silly girl consume his thoughts all these years. He needed to get over this decades long infatuation, and nothing worked better than hard work.

"I'm sure it was only the shock of it. Daniel should have told her." Paul tried easing his frustration.

"I have a feeling that wasn't in his plan," Jesse ground out between clenched teeth. It seemed he had underestimated Daniel Raber after all.

"What ya going to do about it?" Paul asked.

"*Nix*." Jesse shot back. "I'm here to work, earn enough to help *Mamm* while *Daed* pretends I don't exist." Frustrated, Jesse tossed another handful towards the truck. "I can't change how people remember me, how they feel about me, but my mind's made up. I still want a home of my own. This…is home."

"*Goot*." Paul nodded, clearly satisfied.

"Not everyone thinks so," Jesse glanced toward the mill office.

"Perhaps not at first," Paul assured. "But since you're staying put," Paul darted him a lopsided grin. "There's a piece of land, not much more than fifteen acres, for sale a few miles from me. Part of the old horse farm." That had Jesse's full attention. "Family is breaking it apart. The house and some lots are already sold, but it's a nice piece of ground if a man wants a fresh start."

"I might look into it." Jesse wanted to make amends with his family first, before committing to a life in the same community, and there was the matter of money, which he had none of, considering most of his went straight to his parents all these years.

"I know how you've pined over that one. Just promise you won't run off again because of it."

"I didn't pine," Jesse said firmly.

"You wouldn't be so mad if you didn't." Paul ran his thumbs down his suspenders.

"I'm tired of running." No, he wouldn't run. Not this time. No matter how tempting. Seeing the disappointment in Catherine's face nearly dropped him, but Miller's Creek was home.

A buggy pulled in, stopping shy of the office porch. Both friends gazed across the lot and Jesse immediately recognized the man sitting high in the buggy seat, "What is he doing here?"

"I imagine picking Catherine up," Paul said casually. "Did I not mention that part?"

Jesse's features hardened. "No, I think I would have remembered *that* part." Just the sight of Irvin Miller rekindled a mountain of anger. Jesse still remembered the night his path crossed the young woman crying alongside a dark road. He would never forget the look of desperation and of fear for what was happening to her. If Jesse hadn't snuck off, hoping to run into Catherine leaving the bishop's house that evening, he wouldn't have been in that wrong place at the wrong time.

He shook off the odd emotion. Eight years taught a man to look at a thing from different angles. Now, looking back on that night, he saw the blessing in stumbling across the teenager. If Jesse hadn't found Megan when he did, she could have lost the baby and her own life as well. And Irvin had taken advantage of Jesse's unexplained whereabouts, giving his father an excuse to banish him. One lie had upended his world.

Catherine bounced out of the office and climbed into Irvin Miller's buggy. Of all the men she could have saddled herself with, why did it have to be this one? He turned away, refusing to watch further.

"I see I missed all the fun, again," Aiden chuckled, sidling next to them.

"They courting?" Jesse asked.

"*Nee*. Last week he was riding Mollie Lapp around," Paul said firmly. Jesse's friend wasn't partial to Irvin's type either. "He asked Catherine to have supper with his family this evening."

"Daniel approves of their match?" Jesse quizzed. He found it hard to believe Daniel Raber would approve of any man courting one of his daughters.

"She's old enough and got a mind of her own. Besides, it isn't like Daniel can tie her up," Aiden said.

He could, Jesse mused, willing to purchase the rope himself.

"Old enough, huh," Paul looked to Aiden. "Then maybe it's time to tell him about you and M.J.," Paul challenged. Aiden remained silent, surprisingly.

"You're dating M.J. and working for Daniel?" Jesse found that hard to believe. Then again, Aiden always was one for sneaking around rules without really breaking them.

"Ever heard the saying, 'Keep your enemies close?'" Aiden chuckled and then waved off the comment. "I like hanging out with her. She's more fun than you two," Aiden pointed out. "But I'm not sure courting is what you call it. M.J. and I are...complicated."

"Complicated?" Jesse took the liberty of sneaking a glance

at the buggy driving away. He folded both arms over his chest. *Nee*, he hadn't pictured things going this way at all.

Catherine turned slightly, stealing a glance over one shoulder, before turning quickly back around. Did she look back so she could rub salt in his wounds or because she felt his eyes on her? Did it really matter?

"Aiden doesn't know what he wants to be when he grows up," Paul scoffed.

"M.J. and I have been…close, ever since I met her. I love her, but…" Aiden kicked the dirt.

"But what?" Paul insisted.

Aiden reached for a few pieces of scrap wood instead of replying. Jesse sensed Aiden was hiding something and wasn't ready to share it. Jah, things had changed, as things usually did. "Guess you can't blame the man for being overprotective." Jesse said, changing the subject neither friend cared to continue.

"But they aren't *kinner* anymore." Yep, Aiden was indeed hiding something.

Jesse thought of one sister in particular. Catherine wasn't the kind who swayed when other *maedels* tempted boundaries. She didn't try stupid things and had a soft spot for those in need. She alone was responsible for helping Malone Hostetler when reading seemed impossible. At eleven she was smarter than most of the adults he knew and discovered Malone's dyslexia and how to help him.

"*Nee*, they're not," Paul added in.

Jesse thought there was more his friends weren't telling him. The buggy disappeared down the stretch. "I take it you still have sights on a pretty cheesemaker?" Paul shrugged shamefully.

"Ask him how many pounds of Raber cheese he has in his house," Aiden teased.

"I still remember when they moved here and that first

35

Sunday. They looked like frightened sheep being led toward the slaughter," Jesse said unconsciously. Catherine seemed the same defiant girl with pursed lips and chin jutted out, looking determined. She caught his attention then and held it with reverence ever since.

"Rosemary hid behind her *mudder*'s dress for nearly five years before I even knew she had brown eyes." It was clear Paul still held on to his boyhood fascination too. As *kinner*, the three friends joshed how they would marry the sisters, remain friends for life, watching their own *kinner* grow up as they had, together. Life had a way of shutting down expectations and dreams.

"We shouldn't be standing here fancying a future we aren't willing to go after," Jesse said, slapping his work gloves on his trousers' leg.

"So you are here for more than helping your folks," Paul grinned like a cat with a mouthful of bird.

"I might still harbor a few feelings," Jesse smirked. He hadn't spent a lifetime thinking about one woman for no reason, he figured.

"So does she apparently," Paul smarted in return.

"I'm probably the last man on earth she wants to consider, but she doesn't know me anymore. And," he turned his back to the approaching men, "you two need to step up and do your part now, too, or be bachelors forever. None of us are getting any younger, and it's time to start families of our own."

"I'm not sure if being a bachelor is such a bad thing, but I'll tag along just to see how this goes. What do you have in mind?" Aiden rubbed his hands together greedily.

CHAPTER 5

"*You* look nice," Irvin offered as he helped Catherine into the buggy. His smile did much to calm her still frayed nerves. Her encounter with Jesse had rattled her all day.

"*Danke*," she returned, hoping Irvin didn't notice how shaky her hands were. It was all she could do to tally the lumber order. As the buggy turned out of the dusty lot and pulled onto the road, she couldn't help but glance over her shoulder. Temptation or curiosity, she wasn't sure. Sure enough, Jesse was watching. Why was she letting the boy from her childhood rattle her so?

Showing up unexpectedly as he did was enough to rattle anyone. Jesse, the boy who made fun of her shorter hair and her odd accent. If he had known of her past, not being born Amish, she suspected he would have still harassed her. *But he couldn't know.* That secret was only shared with a handful of folks.

Catherine challenged her nine-year-old self by doing what was necessary to fit in when her *mamm* married Daniel. Determination prompted her to be just like all the other girls so not to stand out and draw attention. It had not been easy, changing all that she had known so far, but she embraced her Amish life. Unlike M.J., Catherine wasn't a fan of attention. It had been a blessing that her family hadn't known what they needed. Being Amish included order, rules, and community. God knew how important all three had been for her family.

It was because of Jesse's prodding alone that Catherine learned to speak the Swiss dialect so well. And her hair had grown, as did her ability to do anything any other Amish *maedel* could. She could sew her own dresses by the sixth grade, and no one ever complained at any dish she served. No, no one would ever see her as anything but the perfect Amish *maedel*.

Self-consciously, she reached up and made sure her bonnet was straight, her hair and *kapp* still perfectly pinned underneath. The bishop's fraa often preached that a woman should always keep herself as tidy as her spirits and her home.

Along Miller's Creek, Catherine trained her eye on the changing scenery as Irvin divulged his eagerness for summer to emerge soon. When they reached his home, Catherine accepted Irvin's hand as he helped her from the buggy. She felt no sparks, but *Mamm* often said sparks didn't always come quick, but they did come when you least expected them too. Perhaps she had put too much hope in this evening. She'd not focus on missing sparks but focus solely on enjoying the evening with Irvin's family. This was what she wanted, to be courted by the most respectable bachelor in the community and hopefully find love in the process. Not to be thinking of Jesse Plank.

"Ready?" Irvin smiled before leading her to the front door of the two story house with stone blue shutters. It was different from most of the Amish homes in their community of shutterless windows and upfront flower gardens. Anna Miller preferred gardening in the privacy of her backyard as much as she enjoyed hosting families visiting the area.

Catherine enjoyed a fine dinner of fried chicken, broccoli

salad, mashed potatoes, and macaroni and cheese. Irvin's mother was a shadow of a woman with a mousy voice, but her gentle spirit always made others feel comfortable. Anna also had a talent for making the best macaroni and cheese Catherine had ever tasted, though she would never admit that to her *Aenti* Edith. The bishop's *fraa* would certainly take it personal.

"I'm glad Irvin thought to bring you to supper. I only discovered his interest when he seemed so eager to speak to you during the last gathering," Anna said, handing a slice of apple pie with a perfectly laced crust to her husband, John. "Then he left without a word. It wonders me where you had gone off to."

Catherine tensed at the remark, shooting Irvin a troublesome look. Had he not left Sunday abruptly after agreeing on a walk with her? Then she remembered how quickly his eagerness to spend time with her that day changed when he, too, spotted the newcomer among them. Only it wasn't an *Englischer* at all, now was it. Was it possible Irvin had been just as disturbed by Miller's Creek's returning pest?

"I think Catherine wants your macaroni recipe but is afraid to ask for it." Irvin shot her a wink, ignoring his mother's comment. "She is a fine baker. I've tasted her *kichlin*," he smiled Catherine's way once more. It made her heart swell that he enjoyed them, and she couldn't help but beam under the compliment.

"I'd be happy to write it down for you," Anna said before standing to clear the table. It was obvious Anna didn't appreciate her concerns brushed under the table. Catherine suspected all families had their quirks about them; hers most certainly did, but she didn't like knowing Irvin ignored his own *mamm* so easily.

Standing, Catherine took up her and Irvin's plates and walked them to the sink. Irvin's little sister, Jolene, joined them in seeing all was tidy while the men talked of work at the welding shop.

Once the last dish was dried, Catherine was hoping to visit with the Miller's a little longer, but Irvin already stood by the door with her coat in his hand. "*Danke* for supper," Catherine offered. Anna quickly scribbled the ingredients on a piece of paper for macaroni and cheese.

"Don't forget the paprika," Ann smiled. "It's what makes it stand out so well."

With a new recipe in her pocket, Catherine climbed into the buggy next to Irvin. As far as visits went, her first outing with Irvin had been the shortest she'd ever gone on.

"Thanks for joining us. *Mamm* and my *schwester* seem to be taken with you." Irvin gave the lines a snap, jerking the buggy hard into motion.

Perhaps she was reading it all wrong, another horrid habit she had. He probably just wanted to spend more time alone with her. That was it. She sat a little taller. A nice long buggy ride would allow them a chance to get to know each other better. It was customary, but was she ready for sweet words and...flirtation?

"I have always liked Anna. Your *daed* seemed rather distracted this evening."

"We have a lot of new orders at the welding shop. The Hilty's over in Walnut Ridge are looking to work with us on their buggy business. We can grow. So can they, and all will be happy."

"That's *goot*." Catherine liked that Irvin was thinking of his future. Above them, the sky burned a brilliant shade of red. Sunrise was hard sought for in Miller's Creek, too many hills making morning arrive later than in other areas of the county, but sunset didn't matter how short lived. It was always glorious. "Such a perfect night."

"A little cold still for my liking."

Catherine liked cool spring evenings over the warm lingering days. It didn't take long for Catherine to realize Irvin wasn't taking her on some romantic ride across the county, but straight home. Part of her was pleased, not ready for a long ride under moonlight as her friends described. The other part of her, the one tired of being twenty-four and unwed, was sorely disappointed. She replayed the last two hours over in her head. Had she done something wrong?

When they reached her house, Irvin helped her down from the buggy. "Daniel must be working late this evening." She followed Irvin's gaze to the barn where lamplight flickered through barn slats in the upper loft.

"Our *daed's* both seem to be hard workers," she replied, but wondered what *Daed* was doing in the barn at this hour. Normally he'd be reading his Bible, or helping the boys with their baths. A person could set their watch by Daniel Raber's routine.

"A man with *sohns* like your two *bruders* has his hands and his time full for certain," Irvin laughed. Irvin stopped short of her front door.

"I hope we can do this again," he said, backing away slowly.

Catherine nodded. She did hope they could share another visit. Getting to know each other was the proper way to go about courting. Thankfully, Irvine hadn't tried kissing her. She certainly wasn't ready for that.

"*Goot nacht*, Catherine." He smiled, sending her head spinning.

"*Goot nacht*, Irvin." Catherine hurried inside, closed the door, and then inhaled deeply. With exception of her *daed*, no one felt safe except for the father who wanted her, loved her mother with endless love, and became the umbrella for every storm she or her sisters ever endured, but her first official date was done and over. It wasn't what she expected, but it wasn't so bad either.

CHAPTER 6

*C*atherine pinned her hair into a neat bun and stared into the small oval mirror on her dresser. She looked as tired as she felt. Between thoughts of Irvin and a quick supper that held nothing spectacular, and a pair of dark eyes haunting her, she was lucky to get even a sliver of rest. She lifted her chin. She wasn't about to let Jesse Plank get under her skin again. Not after yesterday's shock at least. She'd deal with the day and not give him a second thought. That's what she would do.

"Irvin Miller." She spoke the name out loud as if doing so would keep her mind straight. He was practical, faithful, and family oriented. So why was she feeling like everything was upside down?

Jesse Plank. That's why. Why had he come back? Was it only to ruin her adult life as well? Catherine hadn't missed a day of work in all her life, but just the thought of working in the same place as her nemesis revived old panics and furies. How many nights had she watered her pillows because of the cruel things he had said to her?

"I'm not a skinny twig anymore, and my hair is longer than

Mamm's now," she told the face in the mirror convincingly and leaned closer. "You're not a silly girl who doesn't know German and cries at the drop of a hat now. This is your home and your life. Jesse Planke will not rattle you." She pointed into the mirror. "You will not shed one tear because of that man ever again. Got it?"

Freshly motivated by her little pep talk, Catherine plodded down the stairs trying her best to feel like she wasn't about to attend her own funeral.

In the kitchen, *Mamm* lifted the morning milking pail to the counter. M.J. insisted milking was her chore, having been so since she fell in love with the duty at a ripe young age, but their mother had found she too enjoyed slipping into the barn in the early morning hours.

"I'll strain it today since M.J. has to be at the market." Catherine fetched the strainer and glass jars in which the fresh milk would be stored until Rosemary was ready to turn it into cheese.

"*Danke*. That will be much help for me today. I've got quilting to tend to and plenty of it," *Mamm* added, with a wisp of light hair clinging to her cheek. Hannah Raber's quilts were becoming something of a commodity at the town's quilting store. *Englischers* paid well for her newest works. Catherine knew her way with a needle, but had to admit her heart resided outside of the home behind the desk where her mind could flourish. Numbers had always been Catherine's favorite of all the subjects in school.

Morning light filtered through the kitchen windows. All four gave a spectacular view of sunrise and a clear shot of the chicken coop Rosemary was currently exiting with a full basket swinging in one hand, her skirt gripped in the other. Her dark haired sister had no idea how beautiful she looked doing something as simple as gathering eggs. Rosemary was the quietest of the lot. Even at twenty-two, Rosemary had no interest in pursuing life outside of the Raber Farm. Catherine had pondered many a night if God would soon send someone who would change her mind. Rosemary would make a fine mamm someday, if keeping her sanity with their *bruders* was any indication. *She needs strength and tenderness, Lord.* A man who understands Rosemary's need for solace.

"I'm surprised you're up and ready so quickly this morning," *Mamm* shot her a sly grin.

"I have a job, and I can't be late," Catherine replied.

"Well," *Mamm* held back whatever thought she had now.

"If you must know...I'm surprised of all the people out there needing work, he hired that one," Catherine spat, straining the milk into glass containers. Probably the reason *Daed* stayed up so late last night in the barn. Guilt did strange things to a person.

"I agree," M.J. seconded, stepping into the kitchen in a peacock colored dress. "Aiden says he plans on staying too." She quirked in that cute way that always earned her smiles.

"How did yesterday go?" M.J. asked before plopping a strip of bacon from the breakfast table into her mouth.

"*Daed* kept him busy, thankfully." Catherine let out a sigh, just thinking about their encounter in the office. Since that uncomfortable moment she found herself struggling with ignoring his presence throughout the day and peeking out the windows to ensure he stayed a good distance away.

"I meant the other thing," M.J. waved a second slice of bacon in the air. Rosemary and M.J. had many common interests. Catherine often felt like a third wheel, considering she didn't share their love for nature and making and selling cheese at the local Amish market. Catherine preferred order and routine. She liked the security four walls gave.

"Oh." Of course her sister was referring to her first date. "It went...well." What else could she say?

"Jesse apparently has experience in mill work. Daniel says

he can grade lumber too," *Mamm* interrupted. Catherine glanced over her shoulder. *Mamm* was struggling with opening a jar of last year's garden beans. Catherine quickly went and loosened the lid for her.

"But why? Why did it have to be Jesse?" Catherine continued.

"Sara needs his help, dear. Eli is not working, so the duty falls on Jesse," *Mamm* said plain and simply. "It is what's expected."

"Since when has Jesse Plank ever done anything as expected?" Catherine threw both arms in the air dramatically. "He showed up in *Englisch* clothes on Sunday. He's been gone all these years. He left them. What kind of *sohn* leaves his family for eight years without a word?"

"I can see he still riles you." *Mamm* lifted an amused brow, and Catherine felt her face immediately turn red.

"He does, and thanks to *Daed* I have to deal with him."

"Daniel needs his help at the mill. You know how shorthanded we've been. You're both adults now, and I'm sure you can find a way to get along."

One of them had grown up, Catherine silently grumbled as she poured herself a cup of coffee.

"He did tease her pretty bad, *Mamm*," M.J. replied. "Remember when he told everyone she had lice and no one would play with her."

"That was a long time ago. He was a boy, just like the boys are now, and *boys* tend to do and say foolish things for attention," *Mamm* said coolly. "Jesse is home to tend to his family and, in turn, is helping ours. It is not our way to judge but to be grateful and forgiving."

Catherine opened her mouth and then closed it again. She was furious with *Daed* for hiring him, with Jesse for simply being here, and with Irvin, who was giving her mixed feelings. Now *Mamm* wanted her to be all grateful and forgiving of the boy who had almost ruined her whole life.

A proper *maedel* would do all those things. Catherine let out a sigh and tried seeing the circumstance through her *daed's* eyes. Help was needed to keep the mill going. Surely she could put forth some effort.

"Martha Jane, be a dear and get a fresh linen set from the drawers upstairs." *Mamm* touched her chin with a delicate finger. "And that thin blue quilt from Rosemary's closet." M.J. didn't question and went straight up the stairs.

"What are the linens for?" Catherine took a sip of coffee.

"Oh, I figure one night sleeping in a dirty barn was enough for our newest hired hand. The least we can do is clean up the loft for him."

"What!" Catherine choked out, spitting some of her coffee out with it. "Are you teasing me now?" *Mamm's* expression didn't waver, proving it was true. Catherine let out an unladylike groan. A horrid sound birthed from years of pinned up emotions, bruised feelings, and nearly forgotten angst. "Please tell me *Daed* didn't give him a place to stay too."

"Oh no," *Mamm* said in her sweet northern accent that often earned her more looks over the years than her *dochtern*. "I did. Sara is my friend, and Jesse is her only child. I just couldn't sleep knowing he didn't have a proper roof over his head. When Edith asked if we had the room, what was I supposed to do, lie to the bishop's wife?" M.J. came bouncing down the stairs, pausing at the look of utter disbelief on Catherine's face.

"What did I miss?"

"Oh, just my life crumbling into a pit of darkness because *Mamm* cannot tell a lie."

"Don't be so dramatic, dear. We were once in need and were given shelter. I am only doing as God instructs."

Catherine had no words to defend herself now. After the death of her birth father, they had been in need, and Daniel

47

had been there to fill that need. Of course her mother felt called to help.

JESSE LAY across the sunken mattress staring up at the spine and bones of the upper barn ceiling. Crumbled sheets lay below him, smelling of spring. He was home to help a family that didn't want him, sleeping in the barn belonging to the father of the one person who still loathed him, but at least the sheets smelled good. Perhaps it was all a mistake, coming home. Then again, God didn't make those, so it must be part of that plan he couldn't see yet. *Trust in the Lord with all thine heart, and lean not unto thine own understanding.* Had those not been words he lived by day to day?

"Catherine Faith," he whispered her name into the wide room and smiled. The woman could hold a grudge, he'd give her that. He came home to face his past, close the painful gap between himself and his parents, and pursue the one woman who had unknowingly followed him across the map. He had broad shoulders and raw determination. He could accept failure, but quitting, that wasn't in his blood. If there was even the slightest chance, even a hint of one that Catherine could forgive him, he would do everything he could to prove himself worthy of her.

A lift of breeze outside stirred what was in the large barn and carried the scents upward. Jesse loved it. It reminded him of simpler days, camping with Aiden and Paul. Hours of mucking stalls, and of Rhett, his horse, a tragedy he had to leave behind, though he carried the regret with him even now. He learned from Paul's letters that his father had sold Rhett to a new family moving into the area, just as he had his buggy. Erasing everything that proved he once existed in his life. He'd never forget that horse and the night he shined and polished that old one-seater for church.

Coming from an abusive home had been hard, especially when watching Catherine and her idyllic childhood so closely. Yet, it had made Jesse want better for himself than the hand given him. At sixteen, he was brazen and felt man enough to court her. So he'd ask Catherine that very day if he could give her a ride home. Her stone cold no wasn't his first slap of reality, but it stung terribly.

Over the years he reminisced about that day. He no longer saw it as a mistake, but a blessing. If Catherine had said yes that day, then Megan and her *boppli* might have not lived. So Jesse trusted. He trusted His plan. God worked in ways a man couldn't understand.

The barn door below squeaked open, and Jesse hurried into a clean shirt. He gave his hair a finger combing and quickly went down the ladder. "Hannah," Jesse greeted. Like her daughter, Hannah Raber possessed a pair of catching blue eyes and locks of honey gold hair that stopped boys in their tracks.

"Jesse," Hannah nodded just as Rosemary slipped into the barn behind her, carrying a stack of fresh linens. The bedding and cot Daniel offered last night had been plenty. "Thought you would need a few things, and I brought you a plate."

"That's not necessary. I've already put you out plenty. You don't have to cook for me, Hannah." She moved closer, setting the covered plate down on the worktable to her right. A whiff of warm bacon sent Jesse's stomach into fits. The growl started out fairly silent then grew into a roar load enough he wished he could eat his words and not appear a liar. Rosemary ducked her head and giggled. Jesse couldn't help but grin. Anyone with an ear couldn't have missed how hungry he was.

"Eat. I can't have you working all day on an empty belly. It's no trouble." He didn't dare protest a second time. It was the Amish way, and one of the simple things about the life he missed most. A warm meal, a dry bed, no endless hurrying about. He didn't feel out of place or intruding, oddly. He felt welcomed. If only he could erase the chunk of time away, but then again without those years, those experiences, he might not have ever changed. He might have become just as hard and stiff-necked as Eli Plank.

When he took up the plate, Rosemary slipped past him and hurried up the ladder like a spider on a web. She always was a quick little thing and still as shy as he remembered her being.

"I'm sorry Eli is being stubborn, but we are all very happy you're home." Hannah said in a soft tone.

"He has his reasons," Jesse replied. Hannah tilted her head and smiled.

"Not good ones," she shot back, surprising him. "God has some work left to do, even on parents. None of us are perfect." Jesse liked Catherine's mother. He barely remembered her, except the way her daughters always surrounded her at the hip. Catherine didn't know just how lucky she was to have them.

"Stay as long as you need. You can join us for breakfast and supper. There's a shower upstairs, too, you can make use of," she added. "Please let me know when you tend on using it though. Don't want to give my girls a fright."

"I don't think eating or showering in your house would make everyone happy." They locked gazes for a moment.

"Well, if you don't eat, you won't survive, and if you don't shower, you'll smell like the dead before you are." She put a hand on her hips. "As a mother of two cantankerous boys, I won't have it any other way." She didn't look like a woman who took charge, but when those eyes narrowed at him, he knew she wasn't without ability. Jesse grinned and nodded.

"I'll eat out here and shower in the afternoons until I get something squared away for myself. *danke*, Hannah."

"Fine, but you remember, I have three beautiful girls, and you are under my roof, even here." He heard the warning loud and clear.

"Understood," Jesse replied respectfully.

"Now is there anything else you need here that will make you more comfortable?" There was one thing that had been troubling Jesse since he arrived home that stormy night.

"Information would be nice." Hannah cocked her head slightly, and one brow hitched. Catherine took after her mother quite a bit. "*Mamm* doesn't look well. You were *freinden* when I left here."

"We still are," Hannah replied, suddenly looking unsure of herself.

"Why? Why does she look a hundred years old?" Had it been the effects of living under the hand of Eli Plank?

Hannah swallowed and lowered her gaze. "She was sick a few years back. The flu, we thought."

A horse couldn't have kicked his gut harder than Hannah's words. The air went out of him. Jesse suspected there were a few reasons his *mamm* looked so fragile, living with his *daed* being the main one, but not sickness. In fact, not once in Jesse's precious memories could he recall her even having a cold.

"Paul never told me." Jesse clenched his fist. "What was it?"

"Few know, and your *mamm* would have never spoken of

such with Paul. Sara wanted it that way. She is a very private woman." His mother had always been a quiet sort. Hannah took a breath and straightened. "They found a tumor inside of her." Still, Hannah's tone remained soft, motherly. Jesse felt his breaths grow more rapidly.

"And?" Why was she hesitating? "I want to know. I deserve to know." Catherine's mother let out a breath. She looked as if it pained her to tell him.

"She went through a few rounds of medicine and a surgery to remove it." Jesse stood motionless, a single tear slipping down his cheek. Like the mother he knew her to be, Hannah stepped forward, brushing it away.

"They got it Jesse, and she is cancer free since her last visit." She offered a half-hearted smile. "That was no more than six months ago. Millie Troyer went with her that time. We each had a turn to go with her. Millie, Edith, and I. Your *mamm* has never been alone through this, I can assure you."

"If she's better, then why…"

"It took a lot out of her," Hannah quickly put in. "Your *mamm* is a very strong woman, and we all see her strength growing every day. Especially since your return."

"You can't know that." Jesse shoved his angry fingers through his hair. Guilt pitted him. If he had only come home sooner, would it have made a difference? He thought not. Eli Plank had made up his mind, found his son unworthy, and few could sway his hard head in thinking different.

"Don't." Hannah touched his arm. "You didn't know, and she didn't want you to. She would have hated for you to worry."

"I would have come home sooner," he replied, wishing his tone hadn't grown so loud. Hannah didn't deserve his anger, but Jesse would have come home if he knew. He would have walked from Wisconsin if only someone had told him.

"It is hard for children to understand why parents keep

things from them, but you are here now, and that's all that matters." Hannah was kind to make light of his neglect. What kind of son wasn't there for his mother when she needed him most?

"*Danke*, Hannah, for being there for her." He couldn't take out his anger on the messenger. Hannah had given him what he needed to know.

Rosemary appeared as quietly as she disappeared. Hannah turned to walk away, and she followed. Before shutting the side barn door, Rosemary peered over one shoulder at him. "I hope you're not the same, because Catherine isn't either."

Jesse heeded a second warning delivered in softer tones. Another reason Jesse had always thought well of the Raber family. Catherine was surrounded by those who cared deeply for her. Jesse was a product of nothing like that.

"I'm not that *bu* anymore." And she was gone. "But what a fool you were, Jesse Plank," he chided himself. "You left them all when they needed you." Tossing the dish towel aside, he swallowed breakfast in a few heavy gulps and aimed for the mill. There was work to be had, and forgiveness to be earned.

CHAPTER 7

"So you helped *Mamm* ready him a room," Catherine said grudgingly at her traitor sister as she gathered up the books and ledgers into her pack and readied for the mill.

"I also left him a new razor from your shelf in the bathroom." Rosemary stuck out her tongue playfully. Last thing Catherine needed was Jesse Plank using her pink razor. "And I took him linens and soap. He didn't even have a blanket, Cat. Just a bag and the sheet he slept on."

"A bag?" Catherine paused, her curiosity piqued. That didn't seem like much after eight long years traveling.

"A Bible, some socks, and a little box." Rosemary fetched a container of milk from the refrigerator, already getting a head start on her cheese making today.

"What was in the box?" Catherine prodded. Snapping her backpack shut, she offered to help Rosemary by fetching the cheese making pot and thermometer while Rosemary gathered her ingredients.

"I don't know. I'm not a busybody, nosing into his personal

things." Rosemary waved a jar of honey in her direction. "You seem mighty curious."

"But you saw a Bible and socks," Catherine reminded her with a lifted brow. "So you aren't against it."

"It was open," Rosemary defended. "We don't know what he's been through, but I don't believe he's here to make your life miserable any more. His folks need help. That's plain to see. Perhaps he's returned to mend what's broken between them and make up for lost time. He may have teased you as a *bu*, but everyone knows Eli Plank has a temper."

That was the truth. If Eli wasn't telling jokes in high volumes, he was scolding someone for not doing things the right way, which was usually his way, and not necessarily right at all. Catherine often ate her lunches alone to simply avoid a headache. Catherine would never wish hurt on anyone, but she had to admit, since Eli's accident, her days at the mill were much quieter. Well, that was until his son returned home.

"Then he should stay there." Catherine hated the sound of her pathetic tone, but it couldn't be helped.

"You think he would be here if Eli allowed for him to return? I overhead *Mamm* and *Daed* talking on it. Eli closed the door on him in the rain. What *daed* does that?" Rosemary began pouring milk into the large pot.

"A little rain never hurt anyone," Catherine said and immediately regretted saying it. When had she become as cruel as Jesse?

"So he said a few mean things when we were *kinner*, but if you haven't noticed, he isn't a boy no more."

Catherine had noticed, but wished she hadn't.

"As I remember it, you use to call him dumb when you beat him in math races. You came home telling me and M.J. about the boy in ratty clothes picking on you. Was that not mean spirited too? The only difference in you saying mean, hurtful things and him doing so, was *Daed* didn't punish you for it."

Rosemary stood upright, a glass jar of milk in one hand, a wooden spoon in the other, and her face as chastising as Bishop Schwartz's when he ran out of pocket candy. Just like *Daed*, Rosemary's dark eyes were capable of making one feel special or regretful. Her sister was the opposite of mean spirited, was as gentle as a lamb, but there were times when she was invested in a thing that her temper surfaced.

"It's not my fault he got punished so often," Catherine finally spoke again.

"Is it not?"

Catherine had tattled on Jesse plenty, their feud lasting all through school, but he had embarrassed her. If only he knew how hard she was trying to fit in. It was true that *Daed* would never lay a hand on one of his *kinner*, whereas Eli had no trouble dragging Jesse behind a barn from time to time.

"I need to go. I'm running late." Catherine clutched her books to her chest, trying not to think too hard on it.

"Then go," Rosemary quipped, clearly not happy to be quarreling with her sister.

"You're right," Catherine offered. She didn't want to quarrel either. Her morning had already suffered enough blows. "I have grown up and should assume he has too. I should've been kinder, too." She lifted the bag to her shoulders.

"I will try to be welcoming, if I must. *Daed* needs him, and I'm sure Eli and Sara are happy he is home."

"*Danke*. I don't like quarreling either." Rosemary offered a hug. "You can't hold grudges. It's not our way. He is just like we were once." Rosemary leaned in and whispered, "Alone and without a home." Catherine was surprised Rosemary even remembered their life before coming here. She had only been six at the time, but she was right about that too.

Catherine pondered her *schwester's* words as she walked over the sunken path to the mill. She'd not let her whole day go sideways. Jesse needed the work and they needed the help.

Who cared about the rest? Not her. "The day is what we make it," she whispered to the wind.

"You're actually living there?" Aiden stood with both arms folded over his chest, a frown on his face. "How?"

Jesse couldn't help but grin at the perplexed expression on his friend's face. "I'm sleeping in a barn, but *jah*. Not sure on the how," Jesse said with a yawn. "Had a full breakfast carried to me as well. Hannah always was a fine cook," he poked just to see if Aiden's face could get any warmer.

"*EE kaw sell nit glauba!*" Aiden shook his head as he pulled on his work gloves. Jesse couldn't believe it either.

"He's charmed," Paul put in. "Always has been. *Mamm* says it's all those pearly teeth." Paul gave Jesse's shoulder a jab.

"That reminds me, can you run me into town soon? I need to get a few things." Namely a razor that wasn't pink, he bit back.

"Sure," Paul said. "I have volunteer classes at the firehouse Friday and Saturday, but we can go today after work. *Daed* won't need me this evening at the shop." Paul's family owned the local tack shop. "Oh, *Mamm* sent you a couple shirts and trousers too. And don't worry, they weren't mine." Paul added.

"You three done chatting like old hens?" Daniel

approached, bringing all the friends to quick attention. "Aiden, you see to helping Vernon run the mulcher today while Paul here catches off the mill for me. And Jesse," Daniel started and then paused, clearing his throat with a short parade of deep coughs. "I think you can restack lumber today."

Jesse didn't dare groan - out loud. Inwardly, it couldn't be contained. Restacking lumber to see boards dried out evenly without bowing was grunt work. Had he not spent eight long years being the new hire already?

"When you finish that, see to cleaning the lot. Those truck drivers have a bad habit of cleaning their truck beds out wherever they park."

Daniel held his gaze, but Jesse didn't waver. If Daniel thought to provoke him with meaningless work, he would be disappointed. With a nod, Jesse strolled off to the secluded back lot to flip boards all day.

By lunch Jesse saw every board turned and restacked. Hannah had been kind enough to carry over a lunch of chicken salad sandwiches, potato chips, and oatmeal cookies. Aiden wolfed his first sandwich down in one gulp, but Jesse savored his. Food had a way of evoking memories, and his own *mamm* had always made the best chicken salad.

It was only when Daniel started coughing again, did Jesse see to finishing his lunch up more quickly. At day's end, Jesse plodded back to the Raber's long after the rest of the hired men had gone home. Daniel insisted he clean the milling area, which meant catching a ride into town would have to wait for another day. A shower and a bed, that's what he needed right now.

After collecting fresh clothes, Jesse knocked on the kitchen door. At this hour he'd not be interrupting supper, but after the long hours he'd put in, he did hope Hannah had saved him a plate.

"Come in, Jesse," Hannah called out.

Jesse stepped cautiously inside. At the family table sat Hannah and Edith Schwartz. At the far end of the table, Catherine's brothers sat eating *kichlin* and coloring. If he wasn't mistaken, Henry, the eldest, was getting more crayon on the table than the coloring book. Something about the pair made him envious. Jesse had always hoped for siblings of his own, and it was a shame his mother hadn't been blessed with more *kinner.* Then again, *Daed* always said he was as much trouble as a half dozen.

"Thought I'd wash up and call it a night if you don't mind." Jesse hugged the doorway.

"Well, let me get a look at ya first." Edith stood and marched up looking just as he remembered. She had always been a healthy woman and full of as much pluck as a pecking hen. The way her eyes twinkled as she took in the whole of him hadn't changed either. Jesse couldn't help but smile. Edith Schwartz was another woman who should have been blessed with a houseful of *kinner* by the way she mothered others. She had a gift for it and didn't let it go to waste.

"You're a foot taller," she said, purposely giving his cheeks a squeeze, remembering just how much he hated it, and chuckled.

"And a few pounds heavier," he grinned bashfully. Edith had a soft spot for menacing little boys. She hugged and fed everyone equally, but it was the downtrodden that piqued her interest most. Jesse was blessed being a recipient of many faithful quotes and slabs of warm cake in his day.

"Glad to see you remember how to dress properly," she pulled him into a hug. Of course she would mention his arriving home in blue jeans and a cotton shirt. Not being baptized, Jesse enjoyed that privilege. Living under Daniel's watchful eye, he quickly remedied that indulgence and dressed as he should.

"All grown up," she continued. "We've missed having ya. It's *goot* yer home."

Jesse hesitated at that. He didn't feel as if he had been missed, but it was kind of her to say.

"You can go on up. The bathroom is to the left, third door on the right. The girls are all out checking the bee hives. I put clean towels in the hall."

"*Danke.*" Jesse unlaced his dusty boots as both boys looked at him with strange interest. He gave them a grin which sent their eyes retreating back to their coloring books before he gingerly walked upstairs. The house was smaller than he remembered. How many nights as a boy had he dreamed of knowing which window belonged to Catherine so he could toss pebbles up in hopes of coaxing her out of the house for a stroll under the moon and stars?

What a fool he had been. Shaking off old dreams, Jesse found the third door on the right and reached for the handle. Suddenly, it swung inward, and there stood a freshly bathed Catherine Faith, smelling of soap and summer, and yes, jasmine. Her blue eyes rounded, but Jesse figured his had too considering neither had been expecting the other. Her damp honey –hued hair hung over her shoulder waiting for a comb to work through it. For once, being in the wrong place at the wrong time was not so terrible.

"Your hair," he stuttered out foolishly. He shouldn't be seeing her, like this, yet his eyes couldn't look anywhere else. She was beautiful.

"Has grown," she smarted with a dash of defiance. "Guess I got over my lice problem." She shoved him aside, nearly plowing Jesse into the wall. Jesse reached out to stop her. They were far too old to still quarrel like kinner.

"I was ten." Jesse met her glare. Her breath spiked, along with her pulse. He could feel it, just under his fingers, the rapid pounding of pumping veins. "Telling you how beautiful you were then, or smart, got me ignored." She smelled like the prairie in the early morning.

"So insulting me was your idea of flattery?"

"Riling you was. Don't you know boys are dumb? Seriously Cat, you can't still be angry at me for what I did as a *bu*."

"Don't call me that," she snapped in return. "And I'm angry for way more than that, Jesse Plank." She jerked from his touch and disappeared behind the closest slamming door. Momentarily shocked, Jesse could only stare. *She probably used up all the hot water too.* Oh well. He certainly desired cold water over his head now.

By the time Jesse returned to the barn, he found Daniel and his boys feeding livestock. That cough was still lingering, by the sounds of things. "I can finish up out here," Jesse offered. He hoped Catherine's father wasn't coming down with something.

Daniel whispered something to Henry, and the boy ran to the feed barrel for more horse feed. "They will show you what to do," Daniel said and aimed for the house.

Jesse turned to the boys. Both an image of their father, with exception of those dark eyes that made it hard to tell if they were up to something or not.

"You really liv'n in our barn?" Henry asked. His straw hat had two holes to his brother's one. Henry was nearly two inches taller, but their likeness was identical.

"For now, *jah*." Jesse pushed the wheelbarrow to the next stall. A bright sunset penetrated the barn, leaving few places for shadows to hide. There were four horses and a pony named Handsome. Jesse figured M.J. gave it the name considering boys didn't use such words. The racket on the far side of the barn were the offspring of three pesky goats Jesse had remembered well. His father laughed for weeks when Caleb Byler tricked Daniel into taking the animals. There were at least two dozen now, and Jesse wasn't sure he would ever get used to sleeping over their nightly racket.

"You scared?" Bryan asked. "I saw a spider this big up there." His small hands span out to the width of watermelon.

"That's big," Jesse smiled. "But *nee*, I ain't afraid of spiders. Now roaches is another matter."

"Where's ya folks? Did they die?"

Henry turned to Bryan. "*Nee bruder*, you can't go asking folks if their folks is dead. *Mamm* would call it being insignificant."

"Insensitive," Jesse corrected.

"We don't know fancy *Englisch* words like that, but since I didn't ask the questions *Mamm* says are insensible, you got an answer?" Henry stood stubbornly awaiting.

"*Nee*, my parents are not dead." Jesse eyed both boys amusingly. "I grew up not far from here. I went to school with your *schwestern*." This one had the makings of M.J. when she was young. Jesse used to hate it when she shadowed along with them so often, asking questions for everything and talking non-stop. Why is the sky blue? Why not purple or green? Why do frogs jump but can't fly? If not for Aiden, Jesse and Paul would have nailed her to a tree until frogs flew in purple skies.

"All of them?" Jesse nodded. Henry forked another scoop of manure. "So was they smart. M.J. says she ain't got any smarts. I reckon so, cause they've yet to know how to tie a *goot* knot in shoelaces?"

"*Jah*." Jesse smirked. "And Catherine was the smartest of all of us." And the most beautiful and kind hearted.

"Told ya," Henry muttered to his younger brother.

Jesse leaned closer. "So smart she didn't have to work as hard as everyone else."

"M.J. says being smart isn't a big deal," Bryan put in, his small hand holding a pitchfork much too long for his stature.

"M.J. has been known to be wrong before," Jesse said matter-of-factly.

"I knew it." Henry kicked a heap of muck and hay. "Rosemary says my brain needs training." Henry stalled. Jesse was familiar with the tactic. More talk, less work.

"She said *you* need trained and your brain needs to stop wandering," Bryan rolled his eyes. "He doesn't like homework or chores. He just wants to fish and catch frogs."

"Well, I for one think fishing and catching frogs is very important, but Rosemary is right. A smart brain leads to less trouble and a whole lot more fish."

Henry's features pinched. "A smart brain can't catch fish."

"*Ach*, it can. Perhaps I could take you both fishing sometime and show you." That earned Jesse two beaming smiles.

"You'd do that?" Henry questioned.

"M.J. says we are trouble." Jesse laughed at Bryan's honesty.

"I bet she did." It seems these two hadn't a clue of the trouble M.J. caused in her day.

"She's sweet on Aiden Shetler, but she doesn't know we know. She kissed his cheek when they were supposed to be apple picking. We didn't tell. M.J. sneaks us sweets and lets us play with the goats." Jesse moved the wheelbarrow to the next stall.

"Rosemary ain't sweet on nobody. I heard her tell Cat she was happy as a bee in honey. I think that means she likes her bees more than getting a husband," Bryan put in.

"I think you're right." Jesse chuckled. He couldn't resist. "And Catherine, does she like kisses on the cheek or bees better than husbands, too?"

Henry cocked a brow. "Cat likes being bossy, that's all. She's really good with numbers, you know? My teacher Nancy says I could learn a lot from her, but I think I'd rather not."

Henry finally figured out how to talk and work at the same time. Multitasking wasn't easy for young boys.

"She isn't any fun either. Can't play a good game of hide and seek for nutt'n," Bryan told.

"Well maybe we should make her practice more. I hear practice makes perfect." Both boys perked at that. "I'll finish up here, and you two get on back to the house so Hannah doesn't worry."

"Say, you want to help us clean the barn tomorrow too?" Both boys waited eagerly for his reply.

"If you don't mind," Jesse said. Henry tapped his finger on his chin as if he needed to think on it.

"Okay then. I reckon you can."

Jesse watched the pair run off and couldn't keep from smiling. Bryan was as honest as Catherine and Rosemary, but Henry... Jesse shook his head and laughed. That one had Martha Jane Raber and mischief stamped in ink on his forehead. After finishing wheeling the manure outside where Daniel composted it for the soon to be planted gardens, Jesse started walking. His parent's house was only three miles away. They may not let him sleep under their roof, but there was also work to be done and plenty of fences to mend.

CHAPTER 8

*A*fter two days of trying to convince his family he was well, Daniel found himself ordered to the bed. *Mamm* rarely made demands, so Catherine knew it wasn't just a case of early hay fever or spring allergies troubling him. "Is there anything I can do?"

"These things must run their course, but when you get to the mill, have Vernon see over everything. He's been there the longest. Your *daed* says he can manage filling orders already sawed. Vernon can handle it."

Catherine wanted to add that she could too, but sensing *Mamm* didn't sound as convinced that Vernon, who had been working for Raber Mills over fifteen years now, could fill the orders, she kept her thoughts to herself. Amish women ran bakeries and sewing shops, not sawmills.

"He thinks he will be right as rain tomorrow, but I'm not so sure." *Mamm* worried her bottom lip. You should warn Vernon he might be needed more than one day. I want Daniel healthy before he takes on the mill again."

"He sounded bad yesterday. I'll get on over there and let Vernon know. We have a load of white oak and pine coming in this morning and an order ready for pick up." Catherine hurried to collect her things. "I heard Rosemary coughing in her room last night. I sure hope she isn't coming down with something too."

Catherine whispered a prayer for both her *daed* and sister as she crossed the pasture and scampered over the hill quicker than usual. When the mill came into view, she stilled. Surely in *Daed's* absence, Jesse wouldn't make a pest of himself. Taking a deep breath and letting it out slowly, Catherine lifted her chin. She was Daniel's daughter. Her family depended on the mill. The workers did too. She could do this. If she could just ignore the aftershocks pressed on her system a pair of dark eyes evoked. Marching purposefully across the mill yard to the phone shed first, Catherine tried not to question why Jesse returned or how he appeared more handsome than she remembered.

Opening the door, Catherine took a step forward and suddenly came to a startling halt at the sight of Jesse sitting at the small desk listening to the answering machine. "What are you…" Jesse raised a hand into the air to hush her.

Hush.

Her.

Catherine narrowed her glare and locked eyes with him while they listened to the soft spoken voice on the answering machine. "Daniel, this is Beulah. Vernon has come down with something and is running a terrible fever. I'm sorry but he can't make it to work today." BEEP.

"Great. *Daed's* sick, Vernon's sick. Who's going to run the saw and see logs unloaded? Catherine threw up her hands dramatically and turned to leave. This was terrible. What was she going to tell customers? "And don't shush me, Jesse Plank," Catherine snapped over her shoulder.

"I'll run the saw today."

"You?" Catherine turned, laughing at the very thought of

him running the saw. "You cannot sit still long enough to spell carnation but think surely to run something with teeth."

"I can spell it now, and it's not hard if you know how to read measurements and have a good set of eyes. "

"Ah, more of your wandering experience," she jabbed, tempted to show him a few teeth of her own.

Jesse moved closer. "I learned a lot while wandering. It's a good thing, too, now that some of it is needed. I give you my word: I know how to run the saw."

"I can't trust your word." At least not as far as she could throw them, which wasn't far. Rosemary was more the throwing type.

"That hurt," Jesse put a hand to his heart. Catherine ignored his dramatics to focus on the real problem here. It wouldn't be convenient, seeing as workers needed a weekly pay and customers needed their orders in the promised time, but she'd simply closed the mill until her father or Vernon was able to return. Yes, that's what she would have to do.

"The men need to work, and so do I. It's just a day or two. I'm running the saw and keeping this going." He lifted two dark brows. "You'll just have to look the other way." He made a move toward the mill.

"You might break something." She brazenly gripped his forearm to stop him.

"Or I might not. Your *daed* needs his rest, and we are shorthanded. That's the only reason I'm here, is it not? He trusts me to be here." He pinned her with a glare, and she folded her arms angrily.

"The only reason, besides *Mamm* being soft hearted." But it was true, *Daed* had hired him. Which still made absolutely no sense to Catherine.

"I've heard some traits skip a generation," he mumbled, his handsome features soured by her sharp words.

"You're not a sawyer."

"You know as little about me now as you did then." He grinned arrogantly. "And since I'm a wayward and haven't taken my baptism, running a loader shouldn't be a problem if these drivers can't do it."

"The loader?" Was he insane?

Ignoring her, Jesse looked about with a glint of seriousness now. "We can worry about the mulching machine this weekend and pile up everything over there," Jesse pointed to his left. "No rain coming, so that'll work. I have a few hundred feet to have cut for the Carpenter order before one o'clock. If you can call the Mackey's and tell them to come tomorrow instead of today, all will *komm* out right."

"We? I don't take orders from you."

"Would *you* rather give them?" he challenged. "I *can* pretend to follow them."

"This is my father's mill. I don't take orders from you." Her temper bubbled to the surface, but Catherine did well to contain it. Jesse always liked to rile her. She'd not let him get under her skin as she had when she was just a girl. She couldn't give him the satisfaction, but the barrier of three feet was quickly broken when he took a step forward. He said nothing, which only irritated her more. This was not the Jesse she knew. Why wasn't he arguing with her?

To Catherine's shock, Jesse reached forward, capturing her *kapp* string between two fingers. Ripples of nerves ran through her.

"We are not kinner anymore. I'm here to help you."

At that, Catherine's mouth opened, but she couldn't find a reply with his nearness rattling her.

"Call the Mackey's. I'll get to sawing logs." Jesse straightened, and the air between them suddenly grew cold.

"Why you?" Catherine asked. Of all the men on the planet, why did her *daed* hire the one man who scared her more than a family secret. "*Ei Ei Ei. Es ish ke fershtant! Ist mad!*"

In a race of Swiss Dutch Catherine erupted in disagreement. By the time she finished, she was winded and exhausted. Adding to her already depleted state, Jesse laughed. Not cold and callous, but as if she simply made his heart happy. The pest.

"Your accent isn't the only thing that's changed," Jesse said before leaving Catherine to stand alone, knowing she still had no effect on him.

"This is the worst day of my life," Catherine growled. Not only was Jesse Plank living in her barn, working at her mill, but now he was telling her what to do. And why did he have to smell like pine soap and sawdust? Was that on purpose?

"Vernon has it too?"

Catherine tried coaxing her father to drink more of the tea *Mamm* brewed in hopes to clear the congestion in his chest. "Jah, but all was well," she said, urging him to take a drink.

Pushing the cup away, Catherine let out a huff. *Daed* was no fan of tea, or missing a day at the mill. "We needed to get the Carpenter order out. He's been waiting for two weeks!" He sounded like a stubborn child with a full belly at the supper table, but Catherine urged the cup in front of him once more, and he finally drank the whole cup.

"There, now yer *mamm* won't think I don't like her concoctions."

"Fairly certain it was Aenti Edith's, but it will help you feel better." Catherine set down the cup and leaned back in the chair she placed next to her father's bed.

"I'm sorry you had to deal with the mill alone today."

"I'm not. I enjoy the work. You know that." She'd not complained once in all the years she'd been there, but he studied her with glassy eyes for confirmation.

"Then I should hope my new hire didn't give you any troubles?"

Catherine stood and went to the window. Though it was nigh on dark, she stared at the plain sunset of blues and grays. "He is shameless and thinks himself *schmaert*," she let out a sigh.

"Always was a cocky *bu*. Joshua talked me into it. You know he and Edith have soft spots. I can see if Joshua can give him work." Daniel moved to rise and began coughing uncontrollably.

"*Nee*, sit back. You're going to cough up a lung." Catherine went to his side. "I'm just being sore, because, well, it's Jesse Plank. But all is well. He actually ran the saw all day."

"What!"

This time Catherine couldn't keep him from sitting up and planting both socked feet on the floor. "Well, Vernon couldn't do it. Needed done," she quickly said, regretting immediately that she sounded as if she was defending Jesse. "Paul said he finished both the Carpenter and Mackey orders in one day." One thick dark brow on her father's face lifted. He probably thought her spinning yarns, but Catherine had never lied to her father before.

"Please get back in bed before *Mamm* comes, and we're both in trouble." Catherine scolded.

With that Daniel slid his feet back under the thick quilts

and lay down. "Well, Joshua thought he knew more than he was letting on. Thinks he's all humble now," Daniel shrugged.

"Humble?" Catherine smirked. A humble man didn't try pulling at your *kapp* strings. "Arrogant, bossy, *jah*, but he can run the saw." She urged him to take another drink, wishing she didn't sound as if she was defending the last person on earth worthy of defending.

"You'll tell me if he becomes a pest? I'd be plenty happy to see him move on." Oh, she could tell him Jesse was a pest, but clearly, her father needed to rest, and she would only be making things harder. The fact was they needed Jesse, and knowing such simply soured her stomach.

"I can handle Jesse Plank. I'm not a child anymore," she winked and kissed his cheek.

"Your *mamm* tells me that Miller fella might be coming to take you courting this evening."

"*Jah.*" She bit her lip. He looked wounded, and Catherine understood why. "It's just ice cream. He owes me a cone." Her father's face didn't shift. "You like Irvin, don't you? I wouldn't dare go if you didn't." Courting was private, but she and her *daed* always spoke openly.

"I just prefer keeping you all little, I guess." He shrugged, making her heart warm. "Your *mamm* is always trying to remind me I can't. *Gott* tends to make all things grow."

"But if anyone could, it would be you," she jested.

"You were such a stubborn child," he grinned.

"But you didn't give up on me." She returned his loving smile with one of her own.

"How could I. I loved you the moment we met." Catherine flushed at his affections. It was sweet watching a grown man admit to such things openly.

"You loved M.J. the moment we met." She pulled his quilt up where it had fallen, noting the chill in the room. "And I don't blame you. She was cute...then," Catherine laughed.

"Rosemary needed you, considering what we all went through, and I was stubborn. I remember everything." She admitted and lowered her gaze. Sworn to secrecy, talk of their former lives had all but faded into the background of the lives they had built as a family.

"Some memories are best forgotten. We cannot live in the past," he said reassuringly.

That was true, and yet she couldn't let all the hurtful things Jesse said those years back be forgotten any more than she could forget she was born *Englisch* and lost her birth father when she was nine.

"But do you remember the day I tried cheering you up, and we went through McDonald's drive through for shakes?"

How could she forget? He had picked her up from school, and she wasn't adjusting to the Amish life very well. Jesse had teased her the whole day, making fun of her accent, teasing that her hair was too short, and then she had to pretend this tall dark Amish stranger was her father. It all seemed like a lifetime ago now. But Daniel never stopped trying to earn a smile from her. He was the kind of man who didn't quit easily. And that day her smile was earned by driving a horse and buggy through the local McDonalds to buy vanilla shakes. It was a turning point in her life. The moment when she realized she wasn't alone in her battles. She had him, her *daed*, at her side for always.

"It's one of my greatest memories. I love you, *Daed*, and don't worry so. I'm not hurrying to run off and marry the first *bu* who buys me ice cream."

"I was the first to buy you ice cream," he corrected. She liked the sound of envy marring his tone.

"Exactly. I will probably never find another like you and die a spinster."

"I guess if I had to let you go someday, Irvin isn't so bad. You know I have always been favorable of Paul. Now that's a fine fella." He shifted and began another round of deep unfulfilling coughs.

"Oh, *Daed*. Paul is like a *bruder* to me. You might want to marry him off to one of my sisters."

"And make the young men of this community think I've gone soft?" he winked.

"Keep it up," she chuckled, "and they will all walk a fine line and make great husbands."

"Maybe that was my plan all along. A father never shares his secrets."

CHAPTER 9

Saturday morning, Jesse breezed through the morning chores for the Raber's and spent most of the morning running the mulching machine at Raber's Mill before heading over to his parent's home. During his last visit, he noticed *Mamm's* garden hadn't been plowed and raked, ready for planting. He couldn't imagine his *mamm* without her garden, and his parents would need what could be grown.

A warm May sun bore down on him as he turned the soil. The feel of the reins in his hands once more brought on nostalgic memories. Summer was not far off. It had always been his favorite season. Between the added work, there was time with friends and less time spent indoors.

"What are you doing here?" Jesse gave the lines a hard yank, forcing both large horses harnessed to the plow to protest. Once under control, Jesse turned to find his father just feet behind him. Both of his father's arms were secured in casts up past the elbow. Those dark coffee eyes were still as beady and close set as he remembered them. Without his straw hat, Eli Plank looked bigger somehow and a lot more bald.

"*Mamm* can't be doing this, and you're in no shape for it."

Jesse replied, still trying to wrap his head around the truth of the *mamm* he thought he knew.

"I can tend to my own," Eli snarled. Jesse gave him a full study. Was this not his family too? *Prideful*, that was what his father was.

"So can I," Jesse returned, ignoring the way his father's face pinched. "You should have told me," Jesse said, staring down at the man who made it clear he didn't have to do anything he didn't want to do.

"I have no secrets, but you..." Eli pointed accusingly.

"I wrote letters. I sent money, but not once did you think to tell me that *Mamm* was ill."

"My *fraa* is my business." Eli spat and turned to leave.

Jesse wanted to climb out of the buggy and force his father to listen. "She is my mother!" Jesse quickly spat, ignoring the buggy pulling up to the barn.

"Who you ran out on," Eli yelled back as an older man began approaching.

"You told me to leave." Need his father be reminded of that night? "I would have never left her if not for you."

"You blame me you left? A man doesn't blame others for his mistakes."

"I take it that I arrived just in time." Joshua Schwartz spoke, and Jesse recognized him then. The bishop removed his hat and gave his balding head a swipe with his forearm.

"I want him off my property, Bishop."

"You don't want your only *sohn* plowing your field when you cannot?" Joshua posed the question, but Jesse could see he was simply taking his time, working up a good sermon to be delivered upon both of them. The bishop had been a witness to many quarrels between Jesse and his father over the years. Sometimes, the sermon was directed at Eli. Sometimes, at Jesse. But none ever healed the heart of what made Eli Plank a man of meanness.

"It wonders me why you would encourage a *sohn* to ignore the needs of his parents. Sara so loves to garden. That is not our way, Eli."

Jesse remained quiet, as did his father.

"A house divided cannot stand," the bishop added.

"Don't I know it," Jesse said unapologetically. "I'll let you two finish this. I've got a field to plow."

"I said leave. You have disgraced this house enough. And don't think I don't know you came back and took *mei* job." Eli turned to Joshua for support. Without full use of his arms, his words delivered less bite. "He even unloaded logs over there. That loader is not for us to use. Daniel knows better, too. The *Englisch* must unload their own logs. Jesse is defiant of our rules, tempting others. He doesn't belong."

Jesse looked at both arms, swollen and hard casted. "Think to take me to the woodshed over it? I've grown, but you are welcome to try."

The bishop shook his head. "There will be none of that today. Eli, let's go to the house and let this young man finish his work." Urging Eli along, the bishop looked over one shoulder and gave Jesse an eerie nod. If Jesse wasn't mistaken, there was sympathy in the gesture. Was it possible the bishop knew what kind of man his father was? Such a thought only fueled his temper further. Jesse gave the horses a slap of the lines and continued what he'd started. None of it mattered anymore, but he would always finish what he started.

It had been years since Jesse felt the chafe of leather on his hands. With his mother's garden ready for planting, he quietly made his way back to the Rabers. Sore hands and a sore heart were both concrete reminders of why coming home was probably not the best idea.

Jesse had seen *Mamm* peek out the kitchen window. He didn't need to see her face to know she was grateful he finished the chore despite his father's dismissal earlier in the day. Sara Plank was always grateful, and that was enough for Jesse to know he'd done the right thing.

No good deed, he recalled the words he'd once seen written on a magnet in a souvenir shop. It was true, not all good deeds were received with gratitude, but good deeds needed done, nonetheless. Jesse's payment was knowing Hannah Raber sought to feed him.

Reaching Daniel's farm, Jesse heard the boys before he saw them. Sure enough, the two were trying to wrangle a large black and white spotted nanny into a corner. He could understand the temptation, and if given a goat to wrangle when he was a boy, he'd probably do the same. Shaking his head, Jesse stepped in and put an end to all the fun. He never had an older sister who might wallop him for mistreating her goats, but these boys had three of them.

It took some coaxing to slow the two mischief makers, and a few secrets about fishing bait, but once the boys headed in for supper, Jesse saw to the afternoon chores of cleaning stalls, giving out fresh water and hay, and scoops of feed for all who lived here.

Daniel's old mare leaned over her stall, and Jesse gave her nose a rub. "It's been a long day, old girl." The polite creature nickered what sounded like thanks before both had their attention drawn outside to the sound of buggy wheels crunching on gravel.

At the barn opening, Jesse leaned against the doorway and watched as Irvin jumped down and greeted Catherine exiting the house. She was dressed in pale blue and looked like a mountain lake in summer. He should be centered on what was important. He needed to bring peace between him and his father, find some way to soften what had been hard for years without holding it underwater. He also needed to prepare for meeting with the bishop and going through the steps of joining the church, knowing his heart was ready and Miller's Creek was home, no matter how some received him. But his mind was swept up in her. It always had been.

How was it that Irvin earned a smile when all Jesse got was the blunt end of her tenacious nature? Watching the buggy leave was another punch to his gut. Catherine made his teeth ache, his hands feel empty, and his heart starved. He couldn't pretend she wasn't part of his returning. *Jah*, he had much forgiveness to earn.

The kitchen door banged to a shut, drawing him to attention. Jesse collected himself as Hannah strode his way, no plate in her hand this evening. She clearly looked distraught. "What's wrong?"

"I hate to ask this of you after you put in such a long day, but…"

"Anything." To be of use, to help another, would help him forget the hunger inside of him.

"I need a few things from town. M.J. is at work, and Catherine had...other engagements. I can't leave the boys unattended." She turned towards the house clearly distraught.

"What needs fetching?"

Hannah pulled a list from her apron pocket. "More medicine. Lots of medicine. I thought it was the flu, but I fear it's also making them sick to their stomachs. It's viral. Rosemary is down now too. If I leave the boys for one second, they'll be next." Jesse doubted that. Those two were immune to anything, he figured, for all the messes they got into.

CATHERINE LICKED at the vanilla cone and tried to put all thoughts of home and work out of mind. *Mamm* insisted she had everything under control. Still, she could have canceled this time with Irvin. Family was much more important.

"You're concentrating on that cone awful hard," Irvin remarked. His chocolate cone had already disappeared.

"Sorry. *Daed* has the stomach flu, and now Rosemary isn't

feeling well. I guess I feel guilty for being out eating ice cream when I should be home helping *Mamm* ."

"I'm sure your *mamm* can handle it. It is her place after all."

Irvin helped her into the buggy and went around the back before climbing up beside her. It was a woman's place to see over her family, but that included Catherine as well, did it not?

"I heard the fence jumper is sticking around." Irvin's glare went to the store across the street. Catherine followed his gaze to see Jesse step out of *Daed's* buggy and jog into the drug store. "Isn't that Daniel's horse?"

"Jah, it is." Deep down, Catherine hoped he too hadn't caught whatever *Daed* and Rosemary had.

"Hope Daniel isn't blind to who that one is. What if he sets his sights on more than a buggy?" Irvin said, taking up the reins. The parking lot was crowded with cars, making maneuvering out of the spot at the back of the ice cream shop a little tricky, but Irvin handled getting them turned around just fine.

"*Daed* sees just fine," Catherine returned before taking another lick of her ice cream cone. *What a terrible thing to say.*

"He's always had a reputation with the *maedels*."

Vanilla ice cream melted over her hand as Irvin continued to talk. Jesse had left at such a young age. He never courted anyone as far as she knew. In fact, Catherine remembered that he once asked her if she would like a ride home, but she had declined of course. Why would she give him the chance to bruise her feelings after barely avoiding him all those years?

"Daniel should stay vigilant. You and yer *schwestern* may have plain looks, but he's not one of us anymore. He's part of the world." Irvin nodded to the yonder. Perhaps he was being protective, though Catherine didn't think herself completely plain looking.

"No telling the things he has done or isn't afraid to do."

Irvin came to a stop at the edge of the road as cars flew by in a hurry to get to where they were going.

Catherine felt a tremor inside her. There was a thin line between her safe Amish life and the outside world. What if Jesse was all worldly now? She remembered well how men without faith and boundaries behaved, and the thought sent a shiver up her spine.

"He'll try taking advantage of your soft hearts." Irvin shot her a warning look.

"My heart is my own, and no one is taking advantage of it." She said with strong independence. No way could Jesse take advantage of something she guarded so closely.

"I hope that doesn't include me. I have been thinking a lot about my future."

"You have?" Catherine questioned.

"I'm of age now. The welding shop is doing well. I can see it," Irvin said.

Catherine's pulse raced as Irvin's blue eyes bore into hers. This was what she had hoped for. A family of her own. So why then did she hear her father so loudly, as if he were standing beside her. *Words may carry a thousand meanings, but it's character that counts.*

Studying Irvin more intently, she wondered just what kind of character he had down under what showed on the surface. "And what do you see?"

His gaze left her to focus on the road again. He gave his horse a slight pull to slow as they drew to an intersection. "I see a big house, lots of *kinner*." He smiled. "Maybe a long haired rascally *hund*."

One that didn't mind keeping to himself, she mentally bargained. Unlike her two sisters, Catherine had never grown fond of animals.

"And you, standing with that perfect smile of yours on the

porch as I return home from work each day." He really was serious. All these years she thought her hair was too short, her figure too thin, and Irvin was looking at her like she was beautiful. Hadn't Jesse told her she was?

Where did that come from? Jesse Plank had no stake in her thoughts. He might have *Daed* fooled into giving him work, *Mamm* too for giving him a roof over his head, but not her.

"I prefer cats and working at the mill," she tested.

He laughed and squeezed her hand before taking up the reins again. "When we marry, you won't have to work in that mill."

Catherine sucked in a gasp. Was this a proposal? Not the way she had always imagined a man asking for her hand. And where were confessions of love? Wasn't that the next stage of courting? Did she want those already, so fast? Peering over to him, his gaze aimed straight ahead, focused on the road and not the words he just dropped into her lap. Her mind was swimming, and she thought she might just get sick. How could he feel love when they just started getting to know each other? It was terribly confusing.

"But I love the mill," her voice clipped. Ice cream forgotten, a warm sugared drop landed on the side of her hand as Irvin began making his way onto Main Street. She quickly shook the ice cream loose from the cone, letting it land on the pavement. Under a red light, they both caught sight of Jesse again. This time he was in the alarming embrace of a woman on the sidewalk. She wore jeans and had long hair. It was the color of Martha Jane's when letting her hair dry in the wind, before pinning it up and tucking it under the veil of her *kapp*. Catherine couldn't see her face, but from what was revealed the woman was *Englisch*.

"Told you. He hasn't changed a bit."

Catherine watched the encounter with scrutiny. A man didn't embrace a woman unless…

"Daniel would be wise to rid himself of that one and fast."

The light turned green, and Irvin slapped the reins with a bit more force than needed. Catherine remained glued to the reunion of sorts until they turned the corner.

CHAPTER 10

"*J*esse?"

The soft voice called out his name as he exited the drug store with a bag in hand. He'd purchased the last two bottles of the medicine Hannah had written down, along with a few other things Daniel and Rosemary might need. He'd learned the hard way that hydration was key with such ailments.

Turning, Jesse noticed the woman standing there. She had blonde hair and wore blue jeans. *Not Amish.* But the smile she wore was part surprise, part grateful, as if she'd been waiting for him, and here he was.

Cocking his head to one side, Jesse dug through his memories. Those were the same brown eyes that once looked at him fearfully, pleading for his secrecy.

"Megan? Megan Fuller?" It was her. The young woman who'd found herself in a fix, and the last person Jesse thought he'd ever see again. Without a care for onlookers, she leaped forward, wrapping two arms around him. Jesse cradled the bags of medicine crushed between them as her over flowery scent filled his nostrils.

Just as quickly as she latched onto him, Megan let go and took a step back. Her face bloomed bright red as she looked upon him with appreciation.

"I told Mom it was you. I'd recognize you anywhere."

Smiling, he said, "Your memory worked faster than mine." She looked nothing like the young woman of his past. It did his heart good to see her healthy and unafraid.

She waved off the observation. "When did you move back to Pleasants County?"

"About a week now. And you, how have you been?"

"Wonderful. Better than wonderful. Oh Jesse, I'm married now. He is an amazing man. I work at the bank here in town," she turned towards the bank, her hair flinging behind her jerky movements. A slight hint of flush was on her face— unprepared to see him after all these years. "That's where we met. He is also the song leader at our church. A very good man."

Jesse was happy for her. She had surely come a long way from the girl who thought she had ruined her life and could never be forgiven. He'd prayed over the years for her, and her child, hoping God would wrap an arm of safety around both of them. A middle-aged woman with short light hair and a stack of books in her arms strode up guardedly and joined them.

"Oh, Jesse, this is my mom, Deloris."

Jesse gave the woman a curt nod. It was good to know she had rekindled that relationship.

"Mom, this is him. This is Jesse Plank." She said it as if it carried great importance. Deloris's eyes went from speculating to beaming, and now they both looked at him as if he had hung the moon. He shifted uncomfortably.

"I am so very glad to finally meet the man who saved my daughter and granddaughter's lives." Deloris extended a welcoming hand.

Jesse took it. "*Ach*, I just happened to be in the right place at the right time." Anyone would have done the same, the way he figured it.

Megan cut in and gripped his arm. "No, Jesse, God put you in the right place at the right time. I would have never survived…without you." She inhaled deep and slowly exhaled. "My life was changed by you. Many lives were."

Jesse's face pinched. He wasn't accustomed to such praise, and his father would certainly disagree with such, but she was right. If she'd been left alone in her circumstances, she'd not be here speaking to him now.

"You were just a boy then, and you knew how bad off I was." A sob escaped her. "You brought my beautiful daughter into the world and saw us to the hospital just in time."

Visions of that night had haunted him over the years. At least now he knew both she and her child were well.

"I still remember the last words you said to me before you walked out of the emergency room."

He couldn't. There were many things about that night he'd never forget. Leaving her in the hands of those who would see her through, he hadn't recalled saying anything. No young Amish man had put himself in such a position before, and leaving as quickly as he could was all he had been thinking about.

"You said, 'There is no distance too far, no mistake too big, that God can't deliver us home.'" She placed a hand on his forearm. "You said He would not forsake me, and my beautiful healthy child was proof of that." Tears streamed down her cheeks. "I would have never called home if not for those words. I would have never joined our church and met Michael. I would not have a beautiful girl who is number one in her class and likes helping others and smiles like the sun, if not for you. You changed so many lives that night, and I will never be able to thank you enough."

Jesse appreciated Megan's gratitude, but that night changed more lives than her's and her daughter's. She'd sworn him to secrecy, and that had changed everything.

CHAPTER 11

*J*esse thought over his encounter with Megan and Deloris all night. Part of him was angry to learn Megan's secret was short-lived and she had reunited with her family. Part of him wanted to demand the years returned to him that forced him out of Miller's Creek. Trying to see things through their eyes, he pushed aside his constant knowledge of being unworthy. *Daed* had told him such for as long as he could remember, but true to his own words, there was no distance too far that *Gott* couldn't deliver you home.

All his life, Jesse had felt a failure. Leaving home had been another failure, but in leaving, Jesse had learned that a man could do the right thing and still not have the perfect family. Individual choice was the cord that severed upbringing. A man could love his roots but had to plant his own. Looking back, Jesse had indeed impacted lives, and not always in a negative way as he first thought.

He needed to put the past behind him. It was time to move forward.

Off Sunday meant there was no church service in their

district. Most visited family on such days, but Jesse knew his family wasn't ready to receive him quite yet. Slipping on his boots, he helped Rosemary and M.J. through their morning chores before giving Henry and Bryan a good lecture about sneaking off to the creek without permission and scaring their *schwestern*. Then Jesse set out to the one place he should have gone to the night he arrived in Millers Creek.

The bishop's.

The beautiful May sunrise rising over Sugar Mountain offered Jesse a tranquil stroll along the road leading to the bishop's farmstead. Trees were bursting with life, and birdsong filled the quiet morning. Spring had its beauties that filled one with hope and newness.

Turning a corner, the old sign came into view, *Poverty's Knob.* Jesse grinned and veered toward it. Since the bishop purchased the farm from the older couple, he never thought to take down that sign.

Jesse took to the slight incline leading to the driveway, and the scent of fresh turned earth and horseflesh grew stronger. In the pastures, Belgians grazed lazily on young grass. They were such beautiful creatures. A hand smaller than a Clydesdale and twice the size of a good saddle horse, their golden coats shimmered in the flickers of early daylight.

Like most young boys, Jesse had dreamed of being a cowboy. For a time, he lived that dream out west and straddled some of the most well-known breeds in the world, but nothing beat the temperament nor the power of a sturdy Belgian.

Any one of the bishop's horses would have been a better choice for breaking new ground for *Mamm's* garden, for as foundered as the land lay, *Daed's* old geldings weren't the most content behind a plow.

On the long porch, he spotted the bishop with legs outstretched, nursing a tall glass of something in one hand and turning the page of a book with the other. "Forgot you bred them," Jesse greeted as he approached.

"Memory has a way of being picky." The elder's gaze lifted slowly, his glasses balancing on the tip of his nose. "Like stubborn old men, forgetting what's most important in life." Joshua rose, sat the Bible in his hands to the side, the glass of tea down, and held out a hand. "Wondered how long it would take you to get here," he grinned cunningly.

Jesse shrugged. "You were expecting me?"

"Why else would I let Edith run off to visit family while I stick around here?"

Joshua was thinner than Jesse remembered. His dark beard had now turned almost completely gray. It was thinner, too, brittle and wiry-looking.

"It was such a fine morning. That's why I figured to wait for ya on the porch." The bishop motioned him to sit.

"How did you know I would come?" Jesse took a seat but didn't lean back. As a boy, how many times had Edith reminded him to sit up straight and not slouch?

"I know the look on a man ready to commit to something. I was betting on it being what we've prayed long for." The bishop darted him a grin. "Yet, I knew you had ground to plow first, so I waited my turn."

"I have plenty to plow yet, it seems," Jesse replied.

"You didn't receive the warmest of welcomings." He reached into his pocket and pulled out two wrapped butterscotch candies.

"It went as I expected." Jesse accepted the candy and popped it into his mouth.

"*Ach*, Eli is a hard man to sway. He was once tender."

Jesse couldn't imagine a tender Eli Plank but said nothing to the bishop's comment.

"It's *goot* you found work, and a roof over your head, *jah*? It may take time, but time is a great healer of hurts."

"Time can also never be measured. It can disappear," Jesse reminded him. He swallowed the sweet butterscotch juices. "Daniel was kind to offer me work and a bed. Though sleeping over a couple dozen goats chatting through the night will take a lot more getting used to." Last night, he had woken to the sound of hooves moving across the floor. Certain he had a visitor in his loft room, Jesse flipped on his battery powered lamp to find nothing moving along the shadows. Of course, goats didn't climb ladders, but they did sound near at hand.

"Daniel may wear a few frowns, but his heart is more charitable than most. Now have you come to speak to me of your faith? Are you of a mind to set down roots of your own, Jesse Plank?"

Jesse chuckled at the bishop's forwardness. He wasn't surprised. The bishop never lingered in his thoughts. If Jesse was truly ready to set down a few roots of his own, then fielding questions wasn't an option this time.

"I am. I came to speak to you about joining the next baptismal classes, though I might choose to live in the next district once *Daed* is well enough to work at the mill again." Jesse had to be honest, and living in a different district might be best for everyone. He and Paul would always remain close friends no matter the miles between them. Jesse would even continue sending money to his folks, and hopefully, he'd be more welcome to see his mother once baptized, but most importantly, Jesse wouldn't have to spend the rest of his days seeing Catherine and Irvin Miller together. Nee, he'd not do that longer than necessary.

"I saw it on your face at the Raber's last Sunday. Many men can listen with the ears while an old minister preaches, but few really hear *Gott*'s words."

Jesse had enjoyed the message and found himself feeling the nostalgia of his upbringing in the sermon. He hadn't known the bishop had noticed. "*Gott* is everywhere, I have learned."

"Even on cranberry farms?" Bishop Schwartz teased. "When I learned you were working for a Mennonite family up north, I worried you'd cut your hair," the bishop laughed. "I'd like to hear of your time there, but another time."

Bishop Schwartz leaned forward in his seat. Jesse hadn't known anyone, aside from Paul, knew of his travels.

"Before I give you your first lesson, I feel it best we put away a decades old question, first."

Jesse let out a long sigh. Of course the bishop wanted to know the truth. Jesse had felt it all those years ago; Bishop Schwartz didn't quite believe Jesse was responsible for stealing the sheriff's car. "You want to know if I stole the sheriff's car and crashed it that night?" The bishop nodded. It was a long story and one Jesse never planned on sharing. He had made a promise to where he was that night, but seeing Megan and learning of her life since then, that night their paths crossed was no longer a secret now that Megan had cleared the air with her parents.

A secret he had kept all these years. If only he knew, he wouldn't have lingered so long out in the world. If he had stayed, how different would life have been for his *mamm*?

Jesse leaned back in his chair and pushed aside the anger of doing the right thing. The impact it had on his life. He no longer had any secrets. He was bending no rules. It was necessary to tell the truth if he wanted to put the past behind him. His future was up to the man sitting to his left.

Staring out over the majestic fields bursting with daffodils, Jesse let out another long sigh before sharing his heart with his bishop. It had felt like a long story, years in the making. The life he lived under his father's roof to the day he shined an old buggy hoping to court the prettiest *maedel* in the community, and from that very public no from Catherine Raber's lips, how life spiraled quickly downward. In the end, Jesse felt the heavy burden of his life lighten, and the story only took a few minutes to tell.

"Catherine was much too young for courting then. That anger is why you ran away that night?" The bishop simply said.

"*Daed* told me I was stupid to think Daniel Raber's daughter would ever care for a worthless boy like me. He did that a lot," Jesse leaned forward, elbows on his knees, and tried not to let old hurts bruise him freshly again. "But *nee*, I didn't run because of it. I left when he ordered me to go." His father would never say a kind thing to him. It wasn't in his nature to be kind, only condescending.

"Eli takes humbling our *kinner* to be kinder adults farther than most. You say you crossed this woman's path and offered her help?" The bishop adjusted his glasses and crossed one leg over the other.

"I couldn't let her walk all the way to town in that condition. She wouldn't have made it."

"*Nee*, you could not. We are to be kept separate, but we are not to leave someone in need either. *Gott* placed you there for that reason. Eli has never told me of this. He thinks it was you in the car that night. He thinks you shamed his house. We all thought so, Jesse."

"I said I didn't do it, but none of you believed me."

"You would not be the first to tell a lie. What were we to think?"

"I dunno. I promised Megan, the woman. She was scared and didn't want anyone to know about her baby. I've never heard so much worry before. She was begging me, while the baby came and screamed at me to promise not to tell. I was just a boy then. It was a lot to take in at the time." Jesse rubbed his hands over his face, the images forged in speaking of the night out loud. Of how one act of kindness had earned him years of pain.

"You may have been a *bu*, but you handled yourself like a man helping her in her time of need. Did the child live?"

"*Jah*. I ran into Megan and her *mamm* in town. She works at the bank and married a man she met there. Her parents took her in after that night." He paused. "Her daughter helps in their church outreach programs and is in the top of her class," he said, strangely proud of that fact. "She wants me to meet her. Her name is…Jessica." Jesse couldn't help but smile and was surprised when the bishop smiled too.

"Perhaps such news might soften your father's heart."

Jesse held back a laugh. "A stone does not get soft."

"Nee, but over time, with enough living water poured onto it, it may."

"You don't understand. I never knew *Mamm* was even ill. I sent letters, money. She could've died. I could have lost her and never seen her again." It was hard not to grow angry in front of the bishop, speaking of his hurts this way, but Jesse had a feeling that's what the bishop wanted from him. Pure openness. "He ushers her inside every time I come near the house, but I see her look out. I'm her only child. I miss my *mamm*. I want to see my *mamm*."

"Sara is a private woman, though some things should not be kept from family and community." The bishop patted his back. "But you listen to an old man when he gives advice." Jesse turned to his elder, desperate for his advice. "You keep going and helping your family. If it takes seven years, or seven more, keep being her sohn."

"Or seventy more." Jesse rolled his eyes.

"Eli will tire of fussing soon, or Sara will tire of not speaking with you. Doing what is right isn't easy. Even Job was tried despite being an upright man, but he endured. He stood fast in his faith."

"My faith was all I had out there," Jesse motioned to the vast landscape.

"Good to hear. Now, what of Catherine?" Jesse coughed at the mention of her name by his bishop.

"I don't understand the question." Or better, didn't understand why the bishop was asking it.

"*Ack*, don't think I don't know it was her that brought you home. I saw how you two used to look at each other."

"You mean how I look at her and how she glares at me," Jesse mumbled, earning him a slap on the back. Who knew the bishop had such a laugh.

"Edith always said it would take a special kind to win that heart." The bishop continued to chuckle in his oddly deep voice. "Have you come home for more than making amends with your family, but to perhaps also consider having a family of your own?"

"She's courting another." He stiffened. "Can't see that changing. I'm a poor man who everyone thinks did horrible things."

"Did you come here for advice or sympathy?" The bishop asked sternly.

"I'll take the advice."

"Smart choice. *Gott*'s will comes with patience. Catherine is a smart *maedel*, smart as they come. Even as a child she took her time to consider things. You know that when trouble comes, she never panics. She uses her head." The bishop tapped his own balding head as he stared over to Jesse. "She has much to offer a man in search of roots, too. Why, I remember the time she jumped from that car and..." The bishop halted in whatever strange direction he was going. "All I am saying is don't think yourself unworthy of a good woman."

Setting aside the bishop's insinuation that Catherine once jumped from a car, Jesse said, "He has finances, a future to offer, and she actually likes him."

"She likes everyone."

But me, Jesse silently added.

"Now, we will start classes today."

"Right now?"

"You got somewhere else to be?" The bishop laughed and stood, and Jesse stood as well. "I don't have a regular class at the moment so this will be a private one. And I don't want to chance you running off again." He slapped a hand on Jesse's back and pushed him inside the house.

CHAPTER 12

*C*atherine didn't like to admit everything at the mill was running smoothly, but as she listened to the buzzing appetite of the saw and the occasional load of logs being brought in on large trucks from Ohio, it was as if *Daed* were at the helm of everything. Jesse not only could handle the saw, but loggers too, and he wouldn't stop smiling every time he passed by the small wooden office.

Pushing aside the gloating of her childhood nemesis and ignoring the way his smile contributed to his fine looks, Catherine tried to focus on her latest lumber order. Best get those all written up before Paul came through the door with another log tally for her to tally. Then there was still the matter of recording the mens working hours and adding this week's numbers to the ledger. It seemed everyone was doing their job, except her. If she could just get her head on straight.

A few minutes into her work, the office door opened, letting in the outside noise momentarily before the door closed again. Pressing the pencil savagely against the paper, Catherine felt his presence, smelled the pine scent of his soap, and refused to lift her head to acknowledge that it was Jesse and not Paul this time. Nearly a full minute went by, and he stood quietly there, unnervingly so.

"If you need something, you best say it. I'm busy."

"I can see that."

Catherine wouldn't let the deep tone of his voice affect her. "You'd rather watch others work instead of tending to your own duties?" She lifted her gaze.

"It's just one of the perks of working here."

Oh, how she disliked this man.

"Your face pinches when you're stumbling over numbers." He dared to smile endearingly. "I don't remember you doing that."

Relaxing her features, Catherine tightened her hold of the poor defenseless pencil, channeling her heated anger. How dare he say such ridiculous things to her? "I don't stumble. If memory serves me, you stumbled over numbers…and words, and simple manners." A sliver of victory lifted on the corner of her mouth, but that only invited him to rattle her further as he approached her desk and maneuvered around the side to stand directly behind her.

Jesse's warm breath fluttered against the exposed flesh of her neck. She closed her eyes, fighting back the shudder of awareness running through her. The scent of freshly sawed logs, workday heat, and man all mingled into a strange and intoxicating mix. Why did he have to be so cruel, teasing her all the time? Why did his nearness have to both warm her and burn her all the same?

"Along with my tongue it seems." He said, sliding the clipboard on the desk. "I always had difficulty concentrating around you." Hovering closer, he added, "You were always the smarter one, but even I know seventy-two and seventy-two are not seventy-two."

Catherine flinched and stared down at her paper. Her confident façade splintered for a second time, knowing she had indeed written just as he said. "Why must you tease me all the time?"

"I'm not teasing you, just stating a fact. Daniel should get you a calculator. It's allowed, and every mill I've been in has one." He rose and took a step back as she got to her feet. The chair scraped loudly against scuffed up floors.

"Yeah, well…" she stuttered, "Maybe they sell calculators at the local drugstore or the diner since it seems to be where you like spending all your time." She wanted to shake him, so thin her patience had become.

"Do I?" Jesse took a few steps back but didn't bother hiding the amusement in those dark ever so unsettling eyes.

"Maybe our barn isn't good enough for the likes of you." A truck backfired outside, and Catherine couldn't help the small sound that escaped her. It was all his fault. Him coming here, stirring her up, ruining a regular day with his manly scents and mocking.

"The loft will do, for now," he dared to smile at her once more. Smile at her.

"Not good enough, you mean, for someone who doesn't stick to one place long."

Where did that come from?

Catherine lifted her chin despite knowing she had said more than she should have. He'd not best her, but part of her didn't like knowing herself capable of speaking harshly. If he didn't bring out the worst of her she didn't know who did.

"I can spend more time…close by…if you'd rather."

"It is none of my business where you prefer spending your time. In fact, I couldn't care less. Less than less. But you did have our buggy and horse, so that is my business."

Exactly. Catherine folded her arms over her chest and stared at him. It wasn't her business if he wanted to court *Englisch* women or not, but as eldest of her family, she had every right to know where he took one of her *daed*'s horse and buggy. *Daed* was sick after all.

"Really?" Slowly her mishandled words pierced him. "Would you like me to promise never to go buy medicine for your father or sister again?" He held up a palm to stop her when her mouth opened. "Just say so, and I will never eat at the diner again. Hannah *should* have to cook me dinner after taking care of her family at all hours of the day and night. I won't even think of being kind and bringing home soup for your sister who couldn't keep anything down for almost two days while you're out with Irvin Miller." His voice scratched her selfish heart.

"Me and Irvin are none of your concern, Jesse Plank." Catherine stuck to her defenses despite knowing how wrong she was.

In two quick strides, Jesse crossed the room at a threatening pace. "I wish it wasn't." His gaze pinned her. Her breath stilled in the mounting heat between them. "He is not who you think him to be Catherine. He is reckless and dangerous and a liar."

"Says the man who wrecked the sheriff's car. You stole and lied about it. Then ran away like a scared little boy afraid of a whooping." Jesse's jaw tightened, forcing the muscles to bulge.

"You have no idea what a whooping is," he threatened. "I hope you never know, though one might do you some good." His eyes took in the full look of her as if tempted to show her. In all her life no one had ever challenged her nerves, her emotions, as he did. Never had he ever looked at her like he was now, either. Disappointed. She felt the unbidden tears and prayed them away.

"You left. You left your *mamm* when she needed you. You teased a little girl who came here scared to death she wouldn't fit in. You burned down a barn."

Jesse flinched at the accusation. Maybe he had told the truth about that one, but did it matter?

"You left everyone that day, like we didn't mean a thing. Like your faith was nothing." Realizing the effect of her own cruelness, Catherine clamped a hand over her mouth to stop the flood of cruelties pouring out.

"I didn't have a choice, and I was only wrong about one thing," he jerked open the door. "You're not the Catherine I remember." The door slammed shut as a tear ran down her face.

"God, what did I do?" Why had she said such horrible things to him? No matter how he hurt her as a girl, she had no idea what his life was like and no right to say things as if she had.

CHAPTER 13

*C*atherine chopped freshly turned garden dirt next to her sisters, Rosemary and Martha Jane. Lifting her head towards a warm breeze that collected the scent of spring across the lower valley, she inhaled deeply. It had been two days since she spoke to Jesse, and she still tasted the bitterness of her own words.

Daed had spent four days in bed to Rosemary's three, but life edged back into something resembling normal, with one exception. Jesse was still there. Well, sort of. If he wasn't working, he would disappear until late in the evening. Avoiding him was not a chore, but Henry and Bryan were becoming enamored, and Catherine didn't want their sweet little minds toyed with. Talk of frogs and fishing were a strong indication Jesse was trying to win them over.

Glancing at Bryan in the center of the garden, a small bucket in his hand, she couldn't stand for it. Her *bruders* need not think to depend on someone from the outside. Jesse Plank was not one of them. He avoided consequences and ran when things got tough. And what kind of man stayed up all hours of the night when he had to work the next day? Catherine only knew of the late hours he kept because her bedroom window gave her the perfect view of how often his lamp burned late into the night. Not that she was looking. She wasn't. This was her home. She was perfectly capable of viewing it.

Giving the earth another stab of the garden hoe, she scoffed. *Jesse Plank doesn't know what the meaning of home is.* He'd not once accepted *Mamm's* invite to supper either. It was rude, but Catherine would not address it. No one wanted to eat supper with dark eyes probing them. It would be hard on her digestion.

Pushing thoughts of Jesse under the dirt, she tried to focus. What a perfectly fine day for planting. *Mamm* says planting a garden was having faith in tomorrow. In these uncertain times, Catherine needed an extra helping of faith.

"Wonder what's keeping Jesse?" Henry eyed the driveway for the third time.

"He could be visiting his folks. *Mamm* says as much," Bryan replied, adding a few more rocks to his bucket. "He promised to teach us a card trick."

Catherine rolled her eyes. *Of all the stuff.* Jesse wasn't teaching her brothers tricks. "It's none of our business where he is. Now keep picking up rocks. We'll never get this done before bedtime if you keep lollygagging," she ordered. Being eldest was a duty not for the faint of heart with *bruders* like these.

"He'll *komm.* Jesse is spendable."

"Dependable," Rosemary corrected. Henry liked big words, but his understanding of them went beyond his five years.

"Ei. Ei. Ei," Catherine added. "It's best you learn now that not everyone is honest with you. *Daed* and *Mamm* won't want you learning stupid *Englischer* games."

"Jesse ain't *English*, and it's not a game. It's a trick. I like tricks."

"We know," M.J. giggled.

"See, you're not so smart, Cat, and just because you don't like having fun doesn't mean we shouldn't," Henry dared. "Jesse is fun, and we like having fun." Henry looked to Bryan for support, coaxing him to nod too.

"He gives piggyback rides," Bryan declared. "And Henry says if we sneak him plenty of *Mamm's* oatmeal cookies, he'll do all our chores!!!"

"I didn't say that," Henry gave Bryan a narrowed look. "He'll be here. He said he would." His dark eyes were testing. Catherine was of half the mind to send all of them to muck stalls and finish the garden herself.

"*Goot*, cause all these rocks are making me tired."

"I guess Jesse's at least made two friends while living here," M.J. snickered behind a dirty hand. Her job was to dig holes for plants, not encourage their *bruders*.

"I don't want to talk about Jesse Plank, or hear about Jesse Plank. In fact, I think it's best none of us speak to him while he's sleeping in our barn. He'll be gone soon enough. He never stays anywhere long." Catherine gave her forehead a swipe of her pale blue sleeve.

"And here we thought you didn't like him." M.J. teased as she dropped a tomato plant into the current hole.

"I don't," Catherine said plainly. "He is not one of us, and we don't need him teaching them tricks."

Ignoring Catherine, M.J. dropped her hoe and took up a second tray of tomato plants. "Jesse will be along shortly." She plucked two from their flimsy plastic pots. "Jesse offered to help Joshua and Edith with some barn repairs. He knows a lot about horses, and with foaling season, Joshua is blessed to have him." M.J. shot a grin towards Catherine as she began dropping plants into the next row of dug holes.

"See. I knew he was busy. He'd not forget the card tricks. Jesse used to work on a ranch with real cowboys," Henry quickly added. Catherine pretended not to care as she dropped jade colored bean seeds in her perfectly straight row.

"He always was a fast learner," Rosemary added shyly. "I thought Dilly wasn't due for two more weeks, and yesterday he told me she would birth soon." And three little spotted bucks born just this morning showed he knew something about goats too.

"Can we go see the babies now? Henry asked. I picked up every rock."

"I did too," Bryan added, not to be left out.

"Sure, but don't go inside the pen. You know the rules," M.J. warned. Catherine continued dropping seeds and carefully toeing dirt over them. She tried not to imagine Jesse Plank as a cowboy on a tall horse, riding across prairies and mountains. Then, she tried harder. All this talk was making her head hurt. She should be thinking of Irvin and that future he envisioned, but all that her mind would let her see was a dark haired cowboy with a mischievous grin. .

"You two shouldn't encourage them. Jesse is not a good example for our *bruders*."

"Is he not?" M.J. rejected.

"Nee, Mollie Lapp told me all about him driving tractors in Michigan, and he even owned a television," Catherine informed her sisters. If Catherine wasn't mistaken, they too were falling for Jesse's charms. "Ivy heard he raced cars out west." A fence post, that's what Jesse was. Part facing one field, another part facing the other.

"Mollie Lapp likes to gossip, and she got that from Irvin, I'm sure. You shouldn't listen to gossip or Mollie," Rosemary said.

"Speaking of Irvin, how did the supper go?" M.J. never held her tongue when a question reared in her thoughts. Catherine gave her an unimpressed scowl. "Oh, come on. We just wanna know if Irvin Miller eats with his fingers or with a fork."

Rosemary snickered at that.

"He knew I fretted over *Daed* and you feeling poorly," Catherine defended looking at Rosemary.

"Right," M.J. said unconvinced. "What about the second date?"

"He talked mostly about a future that any *maedel* would be happy to be part of."

"At least tell us if there will be a third date?" Rosemary asked.

"You can't get to know someone in just two," Catherine replied.

"There are plenty who would be happy to get to know you better. And Irvin has been spending a lot of time with Mollie lately," Rosemary said with a warning look.

"He goes every Sunday with someone to the lake. He and Felty make a habit of it." Being the most social of the lot, M.J knew everyone's business in Miller's Creek, and Catherine immediately believed her. No matter how much M.J. liked to rattle her eldest sister, M.J. wasn't one to tell tales.

"You shouldn't listen to gossip either," Catherine said. "Irvin has no time for foolishness, not with business going so well. You heard wrong."

"Did I?" M.J. cocked a knowing brow. "Irvin Miller is not the man for you."

"And how would you know that?" Catherine shoved a hand on her cocked hip.

"Because the right one for you is closer than you think, and it's not Irvin Miller." Rosemary mocked her stance and lifted a brow.

"If you two think I'm interested in Jesse you are mistaken. He is worldly. You just heard our *bruders*," Catherine's voice squeaked unnaturally. "He plays cowboy and drives, hugs

Englisch women, and he left his family." Both sisters shot her perplexed looks. Ok, so her *bruders* hadn't said all of that.

"Aiden said it was a Mennonite farm. No televisions or tractors. They used those four wheelers like the *Englisch* boys up the road ride on." M.J. plucked a few more plants from the tray and continued planting them. Maybe they would finish before the sun fell.

"I know you think he's up to no good, leaving so often, but you should know, Jesse's repairing his parent's fences. That farm is poorly kept, and though Eli keeps telling him to go, Jesse keeps working, ignoring him. He's trying to do the right thing," Rosemary said believing it so.

That didn't make any sense. "Why would Eli do that if he's helping?" That's what Catherine would like to know.

"Eli is not *verra* kind. He won't forgive Jesse for that car incident. Eight years is a long time to hold anger in your heart," M.J. said and then blew a few pesky blonde curls from her eyes. No matter how thick or long her youngest sister's hair got, she could never keep it contained.

"Is it?" Rosemary shot Catherine a smug grin. "The way I see it, Eli isn't the only one who tends to hold tight to resentment."

"What do you mean?" Catherine didn't like what Rosemary was implying.

"You know what I'm saying."

Like Eli, Catherine also held on to eight years of anger. What did that say about her as a person? Catherine captured her lower lip between her teeth and tried to find a good reason for holding grudges. She couldn't come up with a single one.

"Well, anyhow," M.J. quickly added. "Jesse doesn't have time for much more than sleeping and tricking those two into doing more chores. We can't judge him, especially since we don't know him yet." M.J. looked at Catherine accusingly. She had judged him. Judged him by his past.

"I said awful things to him," Catherine admitted, her voice gone weak. "That first day at the mill and then when *Daed* missed work."

"Then apologize. An easy fix," Rosemary quickly stated. "I think we should put out more beets. Last year they didn't do well," Rosemary said digging through a basket of small jars where seeds were labeled. Catherine was glad for the change of subject. All this talk about Jesse was making her feel worse by the minute. She had done a terrible thing, talking to him the way she had. No matter his teasing, she was raised better and was accountable for her own actions. She wasn't spoiled, as Jesse implied; she was simply thoughtless.

"Are you sure you shouldn't be inside resting?" Catherine said to Rosemary.

"If I lay down any more, I will be so stiff I will never bend again. Besides, the sun feels wonderful." Rosemary lifted her face to the sun and smiled.

"So, Sister." Catherine looked to M.J. "When is Aiden going to officially ask to court you?"

"I don't know." M.J. drew suddenly quiet.

"You've been friends for very long." Catherine and Rosemary passed glances.

"I don't know what is taking him so long," M.J. let out an unladylike groan. "I love him. He's my best friend. He knows all my secrets, all my clumsy moments, and still looks at me like...like I'm the only woman in the world. I tried talking about it and marriage, but he changes the subject every time."

Catherine always knew M.J. and Aiden had stars for one another since they were just *kinner*, but hearing M.J. speak of Aiden in such a way sent a sting of old fashioned envy through her too. Irvin didn't look at her like that, and Catherine was far from any thoughts of love.

"You're blessed to have him. I may be a spinster after all," Catherine clipped.

"What's wrong with that?" Rosemary shot back with a playful grin. It was no secret that Rosemary had no interest in ever giving her heart to anyone outside of their family.

"Are you serious, Cat?" M.J. dropped a plant and went to her. "You're the most beautiful of all of us. You're smart and organized. Your hair never slips from your *kapp*. You never do anything against the rules. Few women can run a business and cook a full meal and sew a new dress in the same day. Any man would be blessed to have you. You take to everything like a new skill to learn. Just like Jesse, there's nothing you can't do."

"I can't hold my tongue," Catherine shrugged. Especially around Jesse Plank. That Catherine couldn't do. "What is one to hope for in a husband? What do you feel is most important?" Catherine truly wanted to know what her sisters thought.

"I'm not having one," Rosemary quickly put in. Catherine believed her. Rosemary didn't trust easily. She was nearly twelve before she had made friends aside from her sisters.

"I want a man who trusts God in everything. Someone who makes me laugh. Someone like *Daed* , who makes you feel safe." Both sisters agreed.

"Safe and loved is important," Rosemary mumbled. "Someone who doesn't push when you're not ready or insists you go places you don't want to go."

"I want to read books that make me think without being frowned on. I want to keep working at the mill, though I know we are to stay home and raise babies." Catherine bit her lip. Reality had a way of shattering fanciful illusions that such a future existed. "I want to do it all," she said wistfully.

"Irvin will never let you do that." M.J. said pointedly. No, Irvin all but said he wouldn't. Life was about sacrifices. If she wanted a family of her own, settling might be her only option.

"I said it's what I want. I'm old enough to know we don't

always get what we want." Catherine wouldn't pretend as a child.

"So you would sacrifice who you are just to have a husband?" Rosemary's question hit Catherine like a bee sting. "Out of all of us, I never thought you would settle so easily. You love the mill and family. There isn't a rule that says you can't have both, Sister."

"Great. Now how did that happen," M.J. raked. All three sisters looked behind them towards the end of the garden. There stood Princess Fiona, the oldest dairy goat, with a parade of friends, munching on freshly planted peppers and what was once bibb lettuce.

CHAPTER 14

*T*he day had been long. His hands were sore. His feet were tired. But as Jesse walked down the narrow country road, he couldn't help but smile. He surprisingly had a fine day working all morning alongside...the bishop. As a boy, he feared the elder with a pungent for candy and eyes that saw the thoughts in a young man's mind.

But it was the last two hours that had Jesse smiling. Helping *Mamm* put out her garden as he had as boy, had done even greater wonders for a man battling for solid ground. Jesse didn't hesitate answering all her questions, though he knew she had clearly not read every letter he had sent her. He spoke of the various communities he'd stayed in and the differences from one community to another. She didn't chastise his time out west on a ranch or little jobs he picked up in between.

It was when she spoke openly about the cancer that nearly took her that he had succumbed to tears. It couldn't be helped. Boys simply cried if their mothers were hurt. He should have been here for her, but as Hannah said, *Mamm's* mountainous faith was what held her together all these years.

According to his *mamm*, *Daed's* injuries were worse than

Paul let on. Two broken wrists, multiple fingers, and a right elbow shattered with little hope for full healing. That changed things. It changed everything. His father still shunned him, but he needed Jesse now more than he ever did. Jesse may have not been there when his folks were both struck down by hardships, but he was here now. "Jesse! Jesse!" The littlest Raber was running down the driveway at full speed. "They're everywhere. Rosemary said to fetch you." Bryan clapped onto his hand and pulled.

Jesse no sooner asked who they were when the whole chaotic scene came into view. All thirty of M.J. 's goats were happily gorging on the entire Raber garden, orchard, and even taking their fill of Hannah's newly budding rose bushes. Catherine looked straight his way with pure displeasure marring her features.

Jesse slowed his pace and started laughing when M.J. pointed a finger and began ordering them all to return to the fields. Like that was going to work. Then again, Jesse wasn't sure what would work. In all the jobs he'd taken on over the years, he'd not handled goats. As if the Lord knew help was needed, a buggy came clattering down the road. Of course it was Paul who appeared just as everything turned to chaos. Jesse waved him into the driveway.

"Problems?" Paul looked to Bryan, then back to Jesse. Never one to ruffle easily, Jesse arrowed a thumb towards the side of the Raber parcel. "Guess you could use a hand," Paul chuckled. "Get in." Jesse scooped Bryan up and put him on the buggy seat before jumping in himself.

"Drop me off at the barn. I'll gather a feed bucket."

Jesse slipped into the barn and quickly filled a bucket of sweet feed. Not their regular feed, but goats, Jesse was learning, would eat anything. Didn't he still have one sock missing? It was crazy to presume, considering he slept in a loft where the only way in was by a ladder, but he was nearly sure the thief slept below, waiting for the cover of nightfall to strike again.

At the edge of all the calamity, Jesse noted the goats were eating more than rose bushes and pear trees. Two were making a good mess of a few dresses drying on the line.

There was M.J. on the verge of losing her temper. Jesse always thought her dramatic and a bit of a pest.

Rosemary was calm, as usual, capturing two cantankerous nannies. If Paul hadn't moved in to assist her, she would have had them too. *Skittish still, that one.* Paul knew that about Rosemary, which is why he paid no mind and looped a quick hand around both chain collars and began dragging the protesting bleaters towards the upper gate.

Near the manure pit, Henry was attempting a bareback ride on one overly fat nanny who wasn't about to accept passengers.

Jesse stood with his bucket of sweet feed and watched amusingly. He wasn't sure who had him laughing harder. Life here was always interesting. Jesse would have stood by watching a minute longer if not for a set of wide blue eyes suddenly seeking him out.

"I don't think he wants back in pasture," Catherine said, backing away from the two hundred-pound Nubian buck that saw her a threat to his freedom. Siding with the buck, Jesse sprang to action, quickly putting himself between both contrary sides. Few people knew just how powerful a buck could be, but he suspected all of Miller's Creek knew Catherine's temperament.

"If he hits me again, I won't be able to run," Catherine said, rubbing the low side of one hip.

"Alright now, big fella, move on along," Jesse gave his neck a push. He knew little about goats, but messing with their horns or their dinner earned you a good head butt. He held the bucket up and gave it a few hearty shakes. And just like that, every two and four-legged creature came to a standstill.

"Thank *Gott*," Catherine breathed out. Jesse tried not to react to her clenching the back of his shirt, or just how close her body was sheltering behind his. "Will they follow you to the fence?" Her shaking voice, her clinging fingers digging for purchase, made him smile. If he knew this was all he had to do to get closer, he'd have left gates unlatched days ago. Biting back a smile, he gave the bucket another shake.

"*Komm* on now. Time to get back on your side of the fence." Jesse led the lot out of the garden and up the hill to the pasture gate that was currently being held open by Aiden Shetler.

"Where did you come from?" Jesse asked as he brushed past him and worked his way into the pasture.

"I'm usually not far," Aiden smirked. Everyone worked together, pushing the small mob forward. "Hi Catherine," Aiden said with a laugh when he noted Jesse's ride-along clinging to him.

"If I let go, I will be alone, and that big one will single me out again. He has never liked me." Catherine upheld.

"I don't mind protecting you," Jesse said amusingly. Her fingers loosened, defiant of the obvious, but she didn't let go entirely. Once secured behind a freshly secured gate, Jesse felt her fingers regain their torturous hold.

"Now we're stuck in here with them," her voice squeaked.

"*Nee*," Jesse poured the bucket's contents in a line over the thick pasture grass and slowly moved away. "Just keep backing up so that buck doesn't smell the fear on ya." He couldn't help himself. When you grew up in an overserious home, laughter was like light and air.

"You're enjoying this, aren't you?" Catherine grumbled behind him as Aiden opened the gate again for them to slip through.

"More than you could ever know." Jesse ignored her groan as he watched the stubborn blue clad *maedel* walking to the right of him as they all made their way back towards the house.

"I got that big one all by myself," Henry boasted. "She won't be escap'n anymore."

"I got two," Bryan added, not to be outmatched. His two-holed hat was completely misshapen.

"You were both very helpful." Jesse patted Bryan's shoulder. "Couldn't have done it without you." Catherine surprisingly smiled when Bryan's brown eyes beamed.

Paul lifted Henry into the air, sitting him on his shoulders. "Go fast."

"I think a ride is plenty today. You're not so little anymore, and I'm tired from chasing goats."

"I guess you want a thank you," Catherine muttered beside him, her eyes focused on her feet.

"A smile will do." Jesse gave her sidelong smile, and in return, Catherine bore a few teeth. "Now that part, I still remember."

A screen door slammed, drawing everyone's eyes to the house. Daniel Raber stood, with arms crossed staring over the whole lot of them. He was six feet of dark and angry looking directly at Jesse.

"Is there a reason my hired hands are here this day?" Daniel's brows gathered tighter until Hannah slipped out behind him and laid a hand on his arm.

"Oh, Daniel," Hannah muttered, but all heard. "Please, come in and have some tea and lemonade. I just made fresh." Daniel looked down on her with a frown, but Hannah Raber didn't budge. Her smile was so large her whole face participated in the action. M.J. wasn't the only one who could steal hearts with a simple smile.

"That would be *vunderbar, Mamm.* And after they helped

save our garden and mend the fence." M.J. rushed towards the house and planted a kiss on Daniel's cheek. "I don't know what we would have done without their help. Every goat was out. They ate half the plants we bought before Jesse and Paul showed up." She turned to Jesse and grinned cunningly.

"Helping was the right thing to do. We were fortunate Paul and Aiden," Jesse quickly put in, "were nearby when Bryan found me returning." Bryan looked up at him but thankfully didn't say a word about Aiden's sudden presence. Jesse patted his shoulder.

"Catherine made *kichlin* and a cobbler last night," Rosemary muttered, and Paul nearly dropped Henry on his head.

"I would never turn down cobbler, *jah*," Paul stuttered. Jesse turned to Catherine, and they passed a long knowing look. It was barely noticeable, the slight tug at the corner of her lips, but she smiled. It would seem she approved of a match with her sister and his dearest friend. No chance she was smiling because he was about to eat a healthy slice of her cobbler. Or was she?

CHAPTER 15

"*W*ell…that was interesting," Hannah said, brushing cookie crumbs off the table into her palm. Catherine dipped her hands into the sudsy water. Under a veil of lashes she glanced out the window as Aiden jumped into the buggy with Paul and Jesse.

Those three had been around most of her life. She smiled, recalling the first time she met them during a gathering, chasing chickens across Minister Graber's yard. Her gaze lingered on the man in the middle. Jesse had broad shoulders under a tan work shirt. He was no longer the skinny *bu* she remembered. She hadn't meant to hide in his shadow, but that buck had already left a bruise, and Catherine wasn't wishing for another.

"I cannot believe *Daed* treated Aiden like a leper."

Catherine rattled back to present at the sound of M.J.'s furious tone.

"He only offered to fix the gates. They obviously need it," M.J. added, setting finished plates down on the counter next to Catherine harder than she should have.

"Careful," Catherine scolded. "Our *bruders* have broken plenty of those already, and *Daed* doesn't need help fixing old latches. He probably thought it insulting."

"And Paul," M.J. shot her an angry glare, her feathers still ruffled. "Was telling him he was wasting his time volunteering at the fire department not insulting? He helps save people and their homes. He's as good a man as any I know!"

"Enough quarreling," *Mamm* said. "Some are just uncomfortable with *Englisch* and Amish working together ever since Sam Fisher helped with that Habitat for Humanity house and ran off with the girl like he did."

"Paul wouldn't do that," Rosemary said in low mumble.

"*Nee*, he wouldn't," Catherine agreed, noting the way Rosemary's cheeks warmed. So Paul had made an impression on her recluse sister. Catherine was of a mind to start coaching Paul on how to win over Rosemary, but she wasn't one to interfere.

"Why is the kindest man ever, the worst when it comes to Aiden?" M.J. said to no one in particular, her mind still on the last thirty minutes of Aiden sweating bullets under *Daed*'s firm glare.

"I think if you three would simply tell him you all have feelings for these good men, he might get over it and learn to accept them. Daniel takes loving each of you very seriously."

With that, three sets of eyes widened and turned to their mother.

"Us three?" Catherine spoke first. *What a ridiculous thought.*

"*Jah*, you three," *Mamm* waved a finger towards each of them.

Catherine gasped as Rosemary clutched two empty glasses to her chest and backed into a corner. Clearly *Mamm* must have taken up the same sickness that had kept *Daed* in bed for days.

"Have you all forgotten I'm courting Irvin, a man who lives

here, and like…lives here?" Catherine stuttered, words failing her. How could her mother think she held an interest in Jesse Plank romantically?

"I don't like Paul like that," Rosemary put in.

"Oh hogwash you two." M.J. turned to Rosemary first. "You think no man can love you or be as strong and safe as *Daed*; well…he's not the only man on the planet. He is our *daed*, and always will be, but Paul is nice and strong and good. I see you sneak peeks at him all the time, and I see the way he looks at you. If you would say one word to him, the man would climb a mountain for you." M.J. turned to Catherine, a shimmer of perspiration on her face. M.J. angry took a lot out of her always merry nature. "And you. You and Jesse quarrel like an old married couple already. If any two people were meant to be together, driving each other crazy for a lifetime, it's you and Jesse."

Catherine opened her mouth to detest such words, but the look on her sister's face distorted into the most pained expression she had ever worn. "Martha Jane, are you alright?" Catherine stepped forward.

"If you two would just stop trying to be coy and comparing all men to *Daed*, you would get married, and *Daed* would get over it and be kind to Aiden. I could be happy too. You both are ruining everything."

In a fit of sobbing tears and angst, M.J. raced out of the kitchen and up the stairs, leaving the women to stare after her.

"She has always been a soft hearted one," *Mamm* said and dared to smirk before turning back to her two remaining *dochtern*. "She has also been the most honest of you."

" I have no interest in *Daed's* hired hand." Catherine lifted her chin and marched out behind M.J.

Hannah turned towards her only remaining daughter, still shrunk in a corner. She moved to take the two glasses from her hand. "I too was afraid," Hannah spoke softly, knowing Rosemary required softness. "Trust is hard to give away, and fear can rob you of joy. Like me, you don't like to disappoint anyone, but I've lived long enough to know when a man loves a woman with his whole heart, and as your *mamm*, it warms me to know each of you are loved. Your *Daed* will come around once he considers the possibility of grandchildren."

With that, Hannah's smile widened as she moved to the sink to finish washing the dishes.

"I CAN'T BELIEVE that *bu* ate nine *kichlin*," Jesse said as Aiden climbed into Paul's buggy beside him.

"Those two could eat a whole cow given the chance," Paul added before clicking his tongue and setting his horse in motion. Jesse tried keeping count of Henry's overwhelming appetite, but he couldn't ignore the way Catherine's cheeks flushed when he told her that was the best peach cobbler he had ever tasted or that his cup had not once gone empty the whole time they sat at the Raber's family table.

"My buggy is just down by the mill," Aiden pointed to where the earth dipped near a flowing creek bed.

"You have been doing this for a while now, huh?" Jesse said with a grin. Aiden had always been the more secretive one of them.

"Most of my life." Aiden removed his hat, giving it a quick study.

"It was nice. A start." Paul set his jaw to hide the smile that Rosemary had spoken to him today. Paul's patience always stood out, but Jesse feared if he didn't try harder soon to let Rosemary know he had feelings for her, he might be waiting a long time yet.

They were smitten fools. The whole lot of them. "You can

run into a fire yet not dare ask Rosemary to sit on the porch with you for two seconds."

"I was trained well to run into fires, not create them. You know Rosemary is...tender." Paul shifted uncomfortably. "Thought we were talking about Aiden sneaking around Daniel to see M.J."

Jesse knew Rosemary was shy, but he never thought of her as tender. Not with keeping bees and helping with all the farm chores as she did. Something about that sister always struck him odd. Like she feared something that wasn't there yet was always waiting for it to appear.

"We were I reckon," Jesse replied, letting the topic of Rosemary fall to the wayside as they pulled next to Aiden's waiting buggy.

"I have a confession," Aiden said abruptly, his unease duly noted. Aiden was the only person Jesse knew who could laugh and frown at the same time.

"Let me guess, you finally asked her to court you?" Paul said.

"*Nee*," Aiden's frown deepened. "I have known Martha Jane most of my life."

"*Jah*, and..." Jesse coaxed. Paul shot Jesse a concerned look before setting his pale eyes back on Aiden as he jumped out of the buggy.

"I love her, but..."

"But you are not in love with her." Jesse could see it now. The boy who shadowed M.J. most all her life, loved her, but not in THAT way.

"She wants more, and I can't give it to her," Aiden said, rubbing the back of his neck and tension growing there.

"You must tell her," Paul said sharply. "It will break her heart if you keep pulling her along. We aren't *kinner* anymore"

"You think I don't know that?" Aiden shot back. "Heck, I

know that." Aiden began pacing, and Jesse climbed out of the buggy to join him.

"That's why you can't tell her isn't it? You can't stand to break her heart." Jesse had guessed right.

"*Jah*. But I cannot court her and marry her if every time I look at her sweet face, I see her like a *schwester*, either." Jesse looked to Paul for help. Aiden had been pondering this for a while. "I thought since Daniel was so protective and the only father in Miller's Creek not trying to marry off his *kinner*, I had time."

It was true. Daniel Raber wasn't like most. Most men hoped their kinner married and gave them grandchildren. Daniel dug in for purchase. Jesse always suspected there was more to their family than most. Secrets he felt he understood, considering Daniel married a woman with three young kinner who could barely speak anything outside of English. He also understood loving something so much you feared losing it. That's why he always looked up to Daniel who was nothing like his own *daed*. Catherine had a strong, held-together family. Jesse never had that.

"I don't want the same things as she does."

Jesse could hear it in Aiden's voice. A young man in search of a different view and new faces. Aiden wanted to leave Miller's Creek.

"I think you should pray on this. *Gott* will help you find the answers." Paul patted Aiden's shoulder. "I do ask you not dally. M.J. doesn't deserve to be hurt."

"She will be hurt," Aiden added painfully. "I know her better than anyone."

"*Jah*, but better now than eight years from now," Jesse put in. He for one knew how keeping the thoughts of his true feelings to himself could hurt those around him. "Honesty is the only way to go here, fellas. We can't keep shying away from what we want for our futures." Jesse turned to Paul. "It's time we stop getting in our own way."

"I did notice Catherine clinging onto you for dear life just a couple hours ago," Aiden chuckled.

"She thinks she hates me." Jesse grinned and gave the dirt a kick. Despite declaring him the last person she wanted to be around, she sure didn't mind using him for cover or smiling at him like he had just lassoed the moon.

CHAPTER 16

For the second Sunday since his return, Jesse once more ignored all the penetrating glares from his father sitting at the second string of tables. The fellowship meal would have tasted better without those eyes judging as they had done all his life.

The Troyer's were the hosting family this Sunday. The multi-generational family orchard delivered a more pleasant atmosphere than most Amish homes with acres and acres of apple trees scattering the family parcel. Mid-May brought forth pink and white blossoms in a full spectacular splendor, sweetening the air. A Godsend to those living downwind of them.

At Jesse's left, Paul sat, finishing off his second slice of pie. To his right, Daniel sipped at his coffee, while the bishop talked about a new foal. Jesse was as surprised as his friends when Daniel took a seat next to him for all to see.

"You should eat and not pick around food like an old hen," Daniel muttered beside him.

"Guess I don't have much of an appetite," Jesse replied,

pushing his plate forward. How was he supposed to eat with *Daed* in clear view?

Bishop Schwartz leaned back in his seat and began stroking his beard as he was prone to do when ready to deliver something of substance. "Daniel tells us you know your way around lumbering mills."

Jesse shifted in his seat, thankful when Silas Graber sat down, blocking his view of his father. "I've done my share of it," Jesse replied.

"He's a hard worker, but tends to hurry through things as if he's the only man out there." Daniel looked to the bishop.

Jesse heard the compliment in there somewhere. "Out there, if a man wanted to keep his job, he had to know how to move his feet."

"I remember how hard the outside world was," Daniel stated.

"Jah, you both have much in common," Bishop Schwartz said before shooting Jesse a grin. "I imagine you have a few tales to tell."

"A few." Sensing his elders' wanted to hear more, Jesse spoke of his years away from Miller's Creek. The better parts of it, at least. The bishop and Catherine's father need not know how many nights he had been hungry or cold.

"Remember when you wrote that you nearly broke your neck?" Paul chuckled.

"A horse and buggy is far less dangerous than a four-wheeler, let me tell you." Both men listened with interest and not with judging. They laughed like friends, like family, and not once had the topic surfaced on why Jesse left in the first place.

"I made good money up there," Jesse continued as he spoke of his time working on a cranberry farm up north.

"It's good you shared half of those wages with Sarah," the bishop said, lifting a knowing brow.

How did he know? Jesse looked to Paul who seemed just as

surprised the bishop knew despite them both keeping that to themselves.

"A man sees over his family," Daniel patted his shoulder encouragingly.

In that, Jesse sat taller in his seat. It was his duty, but to hear Daniel say as much, made it feel more right. Daniel was a man who didn't hand out compliments.

"It can be a chore, having a...stubborn father, but our Father in heaven demands us to do what is right."

"Jah." Jesse wondered if Daniel knew just how hard Eli Plank was, then shrugged off the thought. If he did, Daniel would have never given him a job.

"It earns you a bedroll in a barn at least," Jesse added playfully.

Instead of returning Jesse's playfulness, Daniel frowned as his eyes aimed towards the Troyer's barn. Jesse followed his graze, and he too frowned as he watched Irvin Miller helping Catherine into his buggy. Jesse had hoped to catch a word with her today, offer up an apology long overdue. Just to rub muck into his wounded heart, Irvin glanced toward the house, knowing Jesse would be watching, and grinned like a cat with a mouthful of bird.

Catherine may never learn of his past, or understand what had molded Jesse into the man he now was, but she soon would know who's heart was hers. Jesse knew God had made him for a purpose, and Irvin Miller wasn't going to take that from him this time. It wasn't Daniel that Jesse was concerned with. It was a man who could tell the most convincing of lies.

When Daniel stood, Jesse was of the mind to follow him. Right now was not the time to reveal to his employer that he had been helplessly and hopelessly in love with his eldest daughter since he was a boy.

Daniel was just about to excuse himself from the table when a hand touched his shoulder. As quiet as a moth in the dark, Hannah Raber appeared out of nowhere. "Going somewhere, husband?"

Daniel pivoted slowly, and his shoulders slumped as he looked down at his *fraa*. "Thought to say something to Catherine before she left."

"I'm certain whatever it is can wait for when she returns home," Hannah replied. A lot was said between them as they held each other's gazes. Jesse sat and watched as much more was silently spoken between them before Hannah turned to him.

"Sara tells me you have begun your baptismal classes with Joshua." Hannah's smile brightened. "She can't stop smiling about it." Something about adding to the flock, as the bishop called it, always warranted smiles.

"He must first finish the classes and be baptized before we start patting his back," Daniel said, taking one more glance over his shoulder. "You came home to help Eli and Sarah, but taking classes is a commitment that is life long." Daniel's frown deepened, much like it had when watching Irvin help his daughter into a buggy.

The man could see through ya. Who was Jesse kidding? Daniel knew exactly why Jesse returned. The proof was in the way he was glaring at him now.

"I came home for two reasons." Jesse slowly got to his feet. Paul always said it was best to dive in headfirst. Dipping your feet in cold water took too long to get used to the water. "To make things right with my parents and the second just rode off with another." Jesse quickly collected his black hat from a nearby chair and gave it a finger tip to Hannah before he aimed for the barn, but Catherine was nowhere in sight. Hopefully one of his friends had seen which direction Irvin had gone.

Paul strode up behind Jesse. "I think they went that way," Paul pointed.

"I don't like him being anywhere near her," Jesse admitted. "Why does she have to be so hard headed? I have half a mind to…" Jesse stopped mid-thought and slapped his hat on his trousers leg. "I just told Daniel didn't I?" He looked at Paul. What had he been thinking, revealing to Daniel he had feelings for Catherine?

"Didn't think you had it in you to be so honest," Paul chuckled.

"I wasn't thinking, but eventually I would have to tell him." He just wanted to tell *her*, first.

"You should know Aiden and I overheard the Lewis boys talking before our turn at the table about racing buggies down Sugar Hill."

"So. Let them." Jesse couldn't care less. Now if he could just figure out where Irvin and Catherine went.

"They're racing Irvin," Paul informed, bringing Jesse to a halt. Jesse met Paul's gaze, and his heart sunk in his chest.

"She could get hurt."

Sugar Hill was the tallest mountain in all of Pleasants County, and Catherine was currently thinking heights were just not her thing. Walnut Ridge was not a ridge at all, but a mountain that haloed the valley from her current vantage point. With one hand cradled to her queasy stomach, the other gripped the buggy tightly as Irvin urged his gelding to the top of the steep incline.

Walnut Ridge sat on the most eastern side and was known for its curvy roads, flooding creeks, and a hill that only a fool would think to race over. It was ridiculous. A good Amish man would never take part in such foolishness, she quipped. The Lewis brothers did all kinds of crazy things, and today they had tried coaxing Irvin into joining them. Thankfully he declined, which spoke much to the kind of man he was. Instead, he hoped to take her on an afternoon picnic. While other young folk played baseball in Troyer's front field, Catherine was being courted.

When they reached the top, Irvin veered left, and Catherine's stomach began to settle.

"It's a pretty little pond. Perfect for such a day." Irvin smiled beside her.

This was just what she needed. A remedy to put all thoughts of Jesse Plank out of her mind. Yet, something about knowing he was helping his folks, but they weren't welcoming him home, didn't feel right to her.

Glancing at Irvin once more, she wondered if he was close to his family. She had questions. Three to be exact, that she felt were important in getting to know him. First, was he close to his *mamm*? Catherine found she was more drawn to men who had strong family ties.

Second, did Irvin spend most of his time in the barn, or did he spend his free time with his family? It was silly perhaps. At least her *schwestern* thought all her questions were, but one couldn't simply jump into marriage if they didn't have the same thoughts, could they? It was character she wanted to unveil in anyone she considered having feelings for.

Third, and more personal, how many *maedel*s had he kissed? Her face warmed just thinking of kissing. She knew

Irvin had courted before. Mollie Lapp had told her. Catherine wouldn't hold that against him, but if his lips were frequent visitors on willing occupants as her sister suspected, then she would demand to be taken home immediately. She'd not waste her time on such boys as that.

Like Jesse. He probably had kissed more than his share. No matter, she bit her lip. Jesse was the furthest man from her mind.

A canopy of freshly dressed trees opened. Little pond was an exaggeration. Catherine's breath caught when Irvin pulled into a small field, and a shimmering blue lake appeared. "Oh, Irvin. It's beautiful. Wherever did you hear of it?"

"I've fished here a time or two," he winked.

Catherine noted two more buggies were parked nearby, their horses tethered to trees where they could be shaded from the growing warmth of the day. Irvin helped her down and retrieved the basket in the back of the buggy. Now that her feet were planted firmly on the ground, she couldn't contain her grin. It was something out of a romance novel.

Catherine helped lay out the basket's contents on the blanket. "I have peanut butter cake, and," he dug inside and produced a slice of pie, "cherry." He shrugged handsomely. "Ladies choice." How kind of him to consider her first.

"Peanut butter, *danke*." She offered him a bottle of water, then split the variety of cookies in half so each had their share. It was a simple fare, leftovers from the fellowship meal, but he had gone to all the trouble for her collecting everything. Effort equaled acknowledgment, did it not?

While they ate their desserts, red winged black birds darted between brown dead cattails. The occasional bass rippled the calm lake waters, spurring a laugh out of her.

"Guess we should have brought our poles." Irvin stood and offered her a hand. "Let's take a walk around it." Catherine set down the plastic container with a few peanut butter cake crumbs in it and got to her feet. She slipped her hand into his, his warm, calloused palms scraping against her softer skin. His strong fingers tightened around her much smaller ones. It was sweet at first, but as they began the hike around the pond, his grip didn't loosen. If they walked too far, she might have to ask for her hand back lest she lose all circulation of the tiny digits she relied on for work each day.

"I'm glad you agreed to come." Irvin stepped over a fallen log, seeing her carefully over it.

"Me too. It's beautiful here." Though he walked at a pace that Catherine struggled to keep in time with, she enjoyed seeing the small minnows dart into grass growing in the shallow pond edges. But just like their first supper together, the time was over too soon, and Irvin went to gather up everything to return to the basket.

Catherine saw any crumbs and leftovers were tossed to the birds and closed the wooden lid.

"Let me carry that." Irvin took the basket from her as he looked around as if suspecting someone to be waiting at the buggy for them.

"It wonders me who else is here. We walked around the pond, but saw no one else." There were still two buggies parked nearby.

"Oh, they are somewhere around here," he chuckled as he set the basket in the back, never releasing her hand. If hand holding was this torturous, Catherine wasn't sure she wanted to do much of it. "Lots of couples come here for...privacy. It's kind of a place for such, like picnics and getting to know each other better."

Catherine studied his pale eyes. He'd said that already but his sultry tone deepened, sending a new awareness through her. Catherine swallowed hard when his gaze traveled to her lips.

"You are very beautiful, Catherine."

"*Danke,* Irvin," she muttered, feeling the warmth rising on her face. Irvin Miller wanted to kiss her. Catherine hadn't even got to the part of asking her questions. Was she being too particular as M.J. insisted she was?

Catherine tried to steady her breathing. She hoped she didn't have peanut butter breath. No man wanted to kiss a panting fool with bad breath. *Are you ready to be kissed?* She wasn't sure.

Giggling rose up behind them, and Catherine was grateful for it. She didn't want to refuse her first kiss, but she wasn't sure if she was willing to give it away so suddenly either.

"Like I said," Irvin shrugged. "It's a place for private things," his brows wiggled.

Suddenly the nausea from earlier returned. It was fear, the kind she hadn't felt since she was nine years old and running for her life. It was unfamiliar. She suffered a complete loss of her bearings, and the tightness in her chest began squeezing. Where were the butterflies and warm patters of the heart? This wasn't how it was supposed to be, she presumed, the sudden expert. Irvin's hand reached up and brushed her cheek, and it was then she knew she wasn't ready to give away her first kiss.

"Irvin, I can't," Catherine stuttered and stepped back.

"Saving it for someone else?" His quick reply caught her off guard. "You are just nervous." His free hand wrapped her waist and pulled her to him. He lowered his head, his lips closing in on their mark. Panic arrested her, and Catherine jerked from his hold .

"Irvin, please let go."

"You have been making eyes at me for months. You ate at my family's table. We have been on three dates now. What did you think came next, Catherine?"

Before she could respond that she had no clue what came next, Irvin's lips smacked into hers in a bruising collision.

Catherine pushed back harder, but his hold tightened, sending a new wave of worry through her.

"Well, oh well. Guess we owe you now," the voice laughed from somewhere nearby, convincing Irvin to let go.

Catherine gasped for air and tried to keep her balance, but her head was spinning dizzily. That's when she noticed the Lewis brothers standing near one of the buggies. Two *maedels*, far younger than she, slipped out from behind them. Catherine didn't recognize either one, not even from gatherings from her teen years where youth from all the districts participated.

"Pay up today, and I might treat her to ice cream," Irvin said as if Catherine would consider such an invitation after his forwardness.

"She looks scared," the red head with a lopsided *kapp* whispered to Felty. It wasn't compassion she was offering, not with that grin. Catherine had never felt more out of place in all her life. Lips roughly swollen and feeling very much the center of attention, tears slipped quietly from her eyes as she worked frantically into the buggy.

"Guess she's ready to get back now," Irvin chuckled cruelly.

"You should get her back," Sam Lewis said, and Catherine heard him make a sound like someone gave him a good punch in the gut. All she wanted was to go home. Under the safety of her father's house. She had been a fool to think Irvin was the gentleman she thought him to be. Her first kiss wasn't tender and full of affection. It held no promise of love everlasting. It was bruising and hurtful, and stolen.

CHAPTER 17

"**A**re we just going to sit here in hopes to see them?"
Paul quipped. Jesse knew it was a concern for
Catherine making his friend growl. Paul had always been close
to the Raber sisters, working at the mill, not running off for
eight years.

"You said this is where the Lewis' race is. I'm trusting you
know what you're talking about since I'm the outsider here."
Jesse paced the grassy roadside as Paul sat in the buggy,
wringing his hat in his hands repeatedly. "Whoever would
come up with racing over this should be horsewhipped." The
steep incline was no place for racing at all. "Has anyone ever
died from it?"

"Not from racing, *nee*. A local died here years ago in
winter."

The steep mountain pavement ran from the creek bottom
to the clouds. A four wheel drive would have difficulty traveling
it in the heart of a deep and icy winter, and Jesse had seen
some harsh roads. He took a slow breath, hoping to ease the
pain growing in his chest. If Irvin so much as thought to race

today with Catherine riding beside him, Jesse wasn't sure what he would do.

"I guess we could go up to Secrets Pond and see if he took her there. He usually takes girls up there." Paul craned his neck and peered down the roadway towards a thick patch of cedars.

"Are you kidding me?" Jesse jumped back into the buggy. "You knew he came here often but didn't think to mention that until now? We've been here an hour." Jesse swiped the reins from Paul's hands and aimed the buggy north.

Under Paul's guidance, Jesse followed the little narrow dirt road just a few hundred yards before Felty Lewis appeared ahead of a cloud of kicked up earth. Beside him sat a wide smiling redhead. Felty yanked on the reins, bringing the poor lathered mare to a frantic halt. A second buggy barely had time to stop, forcing the horse to veer off into the thick brush before stopping. Jesse recognized Sam right away. He too had a *maedel* in his company, though this one looked ready to vomit, unlike the redhead who was now protesting the end of what she must consider fun.

A third buggy came to a stop, but the plumage of dust concealed who was riding in that particular buggy. Jesse waited, squinting until his eyes locked onto his target.

Catherine's head hung low until all he could see was her dusted-over *kapp*. She hadn't even looked up when Irvin brought the buggy to a stop. Irvin slowly began backing the horse up a few steps.

"Looks like we got here just in time," Paul said between clenched teeth. Jesse handed over the reins and jumped from the buggy. Behind him, he could tell Paul was already turning his horse around behind him as Jesse marched angrily toward Irvin's horse. Good idea, Jesse thought. They might need a quick getaway.

"You could have gotten us all killed, Plank. What the heck are you doing?" Irvin spit out.

Catherine's head sprang up then as Jesse reached her side of the buggy. A layer of dust covered her dress and apron. Her *kapp* was dirtier in front, but it was her eyes, wild and fearful like a dog in a cage, that sent his heart pounding. Her white-knuckled grip on the buggy frame told Jesse all he needed to know.

"*Daed* said never jump again, but..." she stuttered between tiny hiccups as her body trembled. If there was one thing Jesse knew about Catherine, it was that she feared little. Her faith was as strong as the sea, and as wide as the whole west.

Again? Jesse puzzled. *When had she ever...* He let the comment slide, fearful she was in shock. Protectively, and without a word, Jesse reached into the buggy and lifted Catherine out. She didn't protest. She didn't do anything but melt into him.

"What do you think you're doing?" Irvin jumped to the ground, followed by Felty who joined Irvin to stand in front of him.

"Put her down!"

Jesse tightened his hold and was surprised when Catherine did too and buried her face deeper into the crook of his neck. Coming here wasn't impulsive. It had been necessary. Seeing the fear on her face broke his heart. If not for the circumstances, Jesse would have probably enjoyed holding her for the first time, melted in the feel of her thin frame in his arms. This was not a time for melting.

"Please move aside. I don't want to walk through you." Jesse spoke politely, though his glare left a warning to Irvin. He was no longer the boy who would simply hold his tongue and retreat.

"Daniel will have your hide if he finds out about this." Paul walked between both men and gently lifted Catherine from Jesse's arms. Good ol' Paul. Always calm in any storm, and showing that he, too, was deeply concerned for Catherine's well-being.

"It's fine, Catherine. We're taking you home now," Jesse heard Paul whisper as he carted her to the safety of his buggy.

"Just because Daniel lets you sleep with the chickens, doesn't mean he'll let you eat at his table," Irvin said with a sly grin. .

Jesse ignored Irvin's harsh words. God said turn the other cheek. He had what he came for and was thick skinned after living under Eli Plank's roof. Stopping short of the first buggy and the young girl sitting there and taking it all in with a bemused smile, Jesse gave her one last look. She seemed to have enjoyed risking her life, but Jesse wasn't leaving her there if she wanted an out now.

"You want a ride home?" Her smile came slowly, almost practiced. "We can see you and your friend over there home safe," Jesse assured .

"And miss the fun?" She giggled as a petite brown-haired girl moved past him holding her middle and aimed for Paul's buggy.

"She can't handle fun no more than your little sweetheart," the redhead mocked.

Jesse shook his head disappointedly before locking gazes with Sam Lewis who the *maedel* had been riding with. Sam tossed him a thankful nod. He wasn't such a bad kid. Jesse hoped someday he learned it was best not to walk in the shadows of two older *bruders*. Climbing into the buggy, Jesse pushed aside those remaining there staring at them. He'd learned long ago to help anyone in need, but never let their bad decision affect you. If only he had learned that lesson sooner.

"You going to the bishop with this?" Felty blurted out. Even grown men feared the elders.

"He wouldn't dare," Irvin called out behind him. "No one would believe him anyhow, and if he does, then everyone will know about that pretty banker's *fraa*. The one with a child who carries his name."

Jesse tightened his fist, but kept his head and looked straight ahead as Paul put the buggy in motion.

Paul's home wasn't far. Stopping there first gave Catherine and Sabrina Lapp a place to freshen up.

Jesse stood outside next to Paul, waiting. "Why would she even put herself there," he said angrily.

"She doesn't know him like we do," Paul replied as he lifted a heavy vinyl buggy cover to reveal Jesse's old one seater.

"You could have warned her," Jesse returned and went to see the first and only buggy he had ever owned. "Didn't know you bought it." .

"Got it cheap," Paul smiled and pulled it out of the old shed packed with garden tools. "I don't make it a habit to go around telling folks how to live their lives."

"Just me, then," Jesse added as Paul slipped inside the barn and emerged with a shiny harness. At the nearest gate, he made three clicking sounds. The old bay with one white hoof came trotting up to the gate.

"What are you doing?"

"Readying this buggy for me. You're taking mine."

"Nee, I'm not."

Paul huffed, short on patience. "Catherine will be more comfortable in it." Paul offered.

"It's your buggy. I think this one fits me better," Jesse said, harnessing a mare to a small one seater he once spent all his savings on.

"You are not that boy any longer, and she isn't that girl either. Take the better buggy. You two need to talk." Jesse agreed. "Catherine's pretty tough, but today, well, I have never seen her so…" Paul removed his hat and peered back towards his house.

"Terrified?" Jesse finished and gazed over the farm. The

Eichers didn't farm like most families, having their own fruitful leather shop just a few miles down the road that kept the family rather busy.

"Daniel needs to know," Paul said.

"He will," Jesse replied. Once Jesse dealt with Irvin that was.

Catherine straightened her shoulders as she gingerly stepped out onto the porch. She was glad Paul's family had not returned home yet. How would she have ever explained herself to Thelma Eicher for looking as they did without bursting into tears? Thelma had always been a common sense kind of person, but there was no doubt in Catherine's mind she would go straight to the bishop with today's happenings.

Sabrina stepped out beside her. So quiet she had been while they worked rinsing the stains out of her *kapp*. Her soft brown hair had been freshly pinned, but she continued to wear a ghostly look. What fools they had both been.

"Two buggies?" Sabrina clapped onto Catherine's arm.

There were two buggies awaiting them. Catherine took a deep breath and placed a friendly hand over Sabrina's. "We live in different districts," was all she knew to say as she guided Sabrina toward Paul and Jesse.

"Jesse will see you home," Paul looked to Catherine before turning to Sabrina. "I'll see you back to Locust Creek before my folks return and start asking questions."

Sabrina's hand trembled, still shaken by the day. "Is that okay with you Sabrina? Paul is a wonderful good man and will do as he says he will. I'm sure he would even speak to your family if that's what you want."

Sabrina turned to Paul, hat in hand looking like a gentle giant. His size made him look intimidating, but Paul was the kindest man Catherine knew. Sabrina lifted her gaze and inhaled deeply before giving both of them a nod.

"I'm ready to go home now," she said.

Paul and Jesse muttered a few words between them as Sabrina climbed into the old courting buggy that looked in need of a good washing. Catherne suddenly felt her own hand start to tremble as she climbed into Paul's single seater. Aftershocks, she told herself, ducking her head to whisper a silent prayer of thanks that God sent these two men when He did. She'd put herself and others at risk today. She wasn't one for making such bad decisions, and now she'd have to live with knowing someone could have gotten hurt today.

Opening her eyes, Catherine couldn't help but stare at Jesse as he moved alongside the buggy and climbed in beside her. She couldn't ignore the relief she felt when he'd marched purposefully to her and pulled her from Irvin's buggy. That boldness she had once disliked, mingled with a natural protective nature, surprised her. She could still feel the heat of his anger, despite how tenderly he cradled her. Jesse would never know what today meant to her. She'd never tell him.

"I'll bring the buggy back in the morning before work." Jesse called out to Paul before gathering the reins in one hand.

A surprising calm came over Catherine. A sudden security from the man sitting beside her when so few things in the world felt safe.

"*Bish du base ob mee* for showing up?" Jesse finally spoke as they pulled onto the county road.

"I'm not mad. I thought you were," Catherine's voice clipped in surprise. Jesse had every right to be furious with her. She should've trusted her own instincts, but her desires for love and marriage and a family of her own, had blinded her.

"I'm not. Just wondering what Daniel will have to say." Jesse kept his eyes on the road, but his frown was apparent.

"It's over now. I'd rather not mention it. *Daed* has plenty to worry over already. He need not know I made such a foolish choice if it's all the same to you." Jesse gave her a long look before nodding, and she felt her shoulders immediately relax. Nee, *Daed* need not know she was in a race with the Felty *bruders*.

In the silence that followed, Catherine gazed over the landscape. Spring was slowly shifting into summer, painting all of Millers Creek in an emerald oasis. The clippety-clop of Paul's horse set a rhythm. A heartbeat to the life she loved.

"I miss an open buggy," Jesse said.

"I would think racing cars and driving tractors more exciting, but *jah*, nothing compares to a slow pace on a fine day," Catherine replied, testing the rumors she had heard over the years.

"I never raced cars, but I did drive a tractor from time to time. I take it the rumor mill hasn't changed," Jesse chuckled.

"Tractors are against our *Ordnung*." She lifted her chin, wishing she didn't like the sound of his voice.

"Just a few counties south of here, Amish use them with rubber wheels, but up north, they are metal. For heavy jobs, moving things, not field work. There are communities in Indiana that drive them to work everyday."

"Amish don't drive tractors," she snorted. "And how would you know what Amish from down south or up north do? Did you not live among the *Englisch*?" That was what she had been told.

"I worked for a few, *jah*, but I lived most of my time away in different communities. You'd be surprised at the little differences," Jesse winked.

"I thought you jumped..." Catherine quickly clamped her lips tightly together. Jesse had been kind enough to help her today. She'd not repay him with ridicule and judgment.

"I didn't jump the fence, but I have jumped from one bad decision to another." He lifted a brow.

Catherine noted the sincerity in his words.

"I have never left my faith, but I had to work. Sometimes that meant working for the *Englisch*. In mills, an RV factory, and a large cattle ranch out west." He looked down at her and smiled. "I was even a busboy in a restaurant that only served Chinese."

"Really?" Catherine tried picturing Jesse Planke clearing tables, and the vision brought a laugh to her heart.

"Worst week of my life," Jesse laughed, sending flutters through her.

"I reckon a man should learn to clear a table and clean a dish," she added and grinned shyly.

"I can cook a fine meal when necessary too," he smirked. "Cat, I don't know what all you heard, but I never forgot who I was. I had a different view every year or so, but I never forgot."

Catherine warmed at his admission, knowing Jesse had never swayed far from his faith. That still didn't mean he was living as he should. "Few know that. You've been away a long time." Eight years to be exact.

Catherine remembered the morning everyone in Millers Creek discovered he'd left. She'd pretended not to care. It was Jesse, the boy who stared at her relentlessly and teased her, but inside, she had. She feared she'd played a part in his leaving, until she'd heard he'd stolen a car from the local sheriff. That

Sunday, Jesse had worn a coat too big for his boyish frame, and had driven a different buggy to church. They had never been friends, and on that day, he approached her and asked to drive her home.

Catherine was shocked. She wasn't sure if he was teasing her, or serious. Then Addie Troyer snickered, bringing Catherine to her senses. This was the boy who made her feel small. She told him no.

Now that boy was sitting beside her, driving her home after helping her. Catherine couldn't hep but court the idea of what would have become of them if she had ridden home with him, if she had given him a chance to apologize for the years of pestering remarks. Would their lives have been different if she had?

"I had no choice, Catherine. I had to leave." Jesse revealed, but before she could inquire his reasoning, he added, "Why him?" Two words, but they carried a mountainous weight.

Why Irvin?

"I don't know," she answered honestly, tugging her sleeves downward where Irvin had gripped her so tightly. The flesh there was darkening, and she needed no reminder of that stolen kiss, but now she was feeling the effects of everything. Her sore mouth, her aching hand, and stiff muscles from holding on as Irvin raced down the little dirt road. A tear threatened to slip away in the recalling of it all.

The Lewis brother's laughed as they urged Irvin on. That strange look in Irvin's blue eyes when he accepted their challenge. Catherine had tried to climb out of the buggy before they took off, but Irvin told her to sit still, and she stupidly obeyed.

"The Catherine I remember never did anything she didn't fully think through first." He offered a chastising look. He was right. What had she been thinking? "So, why Irvin? "

"*Daed* likes him, and he doesn't like anybody." It wasn't a lie. "I never thought he would….would…" Jesse didn't need to know about the kiss or the fear that ran through her as Irvin held her hostage in it.

"You chose to court Irvin because of Daniel." He growled under his breath.

"Sounds stupid when *you* say it." She folded her arms and gathered her defenses. Now she felt even more stupid.

"*Nee*, sounds like a daughter who trusts her father. It's admirable, Cat." His words had her sitting a little higher in the buggy seat.

"Well, just so's ya know, his first choice was Paul," she grinned, glad Jesse understood how important her father's thoughts were to her.

"I think Paul has his eyes on another prospect."

Jesse saw that too? "Rosemary?"

"It's plain to see he's always had eyes for her."

"He's never told her though," Catherine replied. Paul was the perfect match for her sister. "I always thought of him as family, ever since that day he stopped M.J. from jumping out of a tree leaning towards the pond knowing full well she was too small to reach the water."

"He's always been like that. You said Daniel told you not to jump again." He gave her a sidelong look. "Are you saying you actually jumped from a buggy before?"

"Oh," Catherine flinched. She'd promised to never speak of her past, and in a moment of panic, let the words slip. "I… well…might have jumped out of a car once." His brows both raised in unison.

"A car?"

"It was a long time ago, and necessary. I'm not foolish," her voice hiked. No way Jesse could understand her family's secret. "I don't want to talk about it."

"Okay." She was relieved he seemed to understand her

reluctance to speak of it. "Another time, perhaps, you can tell me."

Fat chance. She and her sisters all promised never to speak of the day she was kidnapped, or the reason behind them moving to Millers Creek. The past was the past, and it belonged there in that place; forgotten.

"Catherine, where did you live before?"

"I don't want to talk about that either," she replied sternly.

"Very well," Jesse said . "We can add it to the list of *another time.*"

He wanted there to be another time. Stunned, Catherine couldn't understand why he would. She had not been kind to him when her father gave him work or a place to sleep.

"*Danke* for today. I don't know how you and Paul knew where I was, but *danke,* Jesse."

"No thanks needed, but please don't trust Irvin." Jesse said as he pulled the buggy up next to her porch.

It was a truce, a momentary one after two decades of finding each other intolerable.

"I still don't like you," she said, slipping out of the buggy. When he met her smile with his own, she knew she was in trouble. *"Out of the frying pan and into the fire."* Isn't that what Edith would say?

"That's okay too, for now. We will soon remedy that list."

Jesse drove the buggy toward the barn, leaving Catherine standing in the driveway and for the second time she felt it. Butterflies.

CHAPTER 18

*J*une grew boldly warm. It had been two weeks since Catherine made the mistake of climbing in a buggy with Irvin Miller. Two weeks since discovering it was hard not to find Jesse Plank...interesting.

With M.J. helping at the Troyers' today and Rosemary elbow-deep in cheesemaking, Catherine decided to take one of her rare strolls to the creek. It was the perfect spot for thinking as she'd learned the first time *Daed* introduced it to her.

The gurgle of soft currents offered a calm that gave a woman time to ponder. Jesse hadn't mentioned anything to her *daed*. Instead, he spent that evening, and those following, playing with her young *bruders*. Baseball, hoops. Jesse could even turn milking goats into a game to M.J.'s delight. Henry and Bryan shadowed him everywhere, and whatever Jesse said was truth. *Mamm* appreciated knowing there was another set of eyes on them, considering Henry and Bryan tended to bore easily and get into mischief often. Jesse was obviously immune to their tactics.

Yesterday, Jesse finally accepted *Mamm's* invitation to

supper. He ate heartily, but who could resist Rosemary's sage chicken and dressing. He wasn't the boy she remembered at all, and Catherine was fully aware of the growing attraction between them. It was confusing. She had not liked him for so long, she wasn't sure if she should.

Finding a seat on a nearby log, Catherine let out a frustrated breath as water rippled over three large stones before her. "What am I to do, Lord? I have made such a mess of things. I cannot be trusted to even know my own heart," she whispered into the wind.

"I hear a broom does wonders to remedy a mess."

Catherine startled to her feet. No one outside of her family ever came here. "I thought I was alone."

"So did I." Jesse rose from his perch just a few yards downstream and slowly walked her way. His hair had grown since that first morning he had stepped into the mill office. It's black as night shade was softened, not dangerous or prickly at all. He wore a crisp minty green shirt, suspenders overlapped, both moving in accordance to his muscular build. Long legs, now solid, not ready to run, covered much more ground in fewer steps than she could on her stickly two. No man could stir the woman in her like he could, like he always could, and she wasn't sure how she felt about that.

"I'll go." She hated the sound of shattering in her voice.

"Or I'll go, and you can stay." Those dark eyes penetrated her indecision. Seconds waned. Water searched for new scenery. Birds chirped evening calls. A rustling downstream, a squirrel perhaps considering so many ran around here, didn't tempt them to look away. It was the same game of their youth, neither daring to blink, breaking contact. She wouldn't let him win back then, yet now it all seemed so silly, and she lowered her gaze.

"I win, again," Jesse said mockingly.

"Oh, you are ridiculous," Catherine barked and turned to leave him to his silly games.

"Don't go."

Facing him once more, Catherine narrowed her gaze and lifted her chin. Jesse reached out, and she took a step back.

"*Komm*, Catherine. Tell me what has you out of sorts."

"I'm mad." She was mad. Mad that he was smiling and confusing her heart. "You come home after all these years and mess everything up."

"It's my home. You know my folks need me even if they don't want me, and how else could I see you again?"

"Me?" Catherine's laugh couldn't be contained. "I'm just one of the girls you made cry, and if you think I have an interest in you and your handsome smile, you're wrong."

"You find me handsome, Catherine Faith?"

"You…" Was there no end to his teasing? Taking another step back, Jesse reached out and gripped her upper arm.

"Let me go, Jesse Plank." Yanking from his grasp, he smiled and did exactly what she asked. It took only a breath for Catherine to realize her mistake as she went sailing backward without land or rock left to stand on.

The water was cold, and when Catherine surfaced, she sputtered out a mouthful of creek water. Blinking back droplets, she could see Jesse standing on the bank. This time no smile mocked her in his eyes.

"Feel better?" Jesse cocked his head and crossed his arms.

Neither his fine looks or her over reaction made her any drier, warmer, or smarter. Catherine simply stared. If the roles were reversed, she would have let him go too.

"Your *kapp* is crooked," he smirked, knowing how it would affect her. He offered her a hand up. She studied his offering, testing its trustworthiness, before reaching up and placing a hand in his. Calculating her next move, she waited for the right moment. With a smile, Catherine held out her free hand, implying she needed extra assistance, and he played into the vulnerable fragility she wore in her features.

Planting both feet firmly apart, Jesse gripped her other hand and began to pull her out of the water. The man should have never let his guard down. Pulling against him, Catherine yanked hard, knocking him off balance. Jesse tittered before he went sailing over Catherine's head and into the water with an enormous splash.

Jesse came up much more gracefully than he went in, and those eyes scored her heart. Seeing him sent a shiver over her. Feeling the fast pace of heart couldn't be ignored, and in that moment of trickling water and a bobwhite's call, Catherine knew he saw her too.

JESSE WIPED the hair from his eyes. This was the Catherine he missed. The one he carried in his heart across the map.

"You played right into my hand." She burst into laughter, either by the look of him, or for the pun she'd delivered.

Her laughter sent a surge of awakening through him. Jesse lifted a long strand of hair clinging to her cheek and brushed it behind her ear. "If I knew a way," he swallowed the lump in his throat. He wanted to be patient. "to grab hold of a day, a moment, and make it stand still." Her breaths quickened as fear flashed over her expression.

"Let's get you out of here," he said, knowing she wasn't a fan of surprises. He had a few for her, but those could wait. There was time. Helping her back to dry land, Jesse couldn't help but notice her wince.

"Are you hurt?"

"Nee, are you?" she asked, yanking her sleeves down

suspiciously. She's the only woman he knew who would argue with a tree.

"Let me see." Pulling up her sleeve, the ring of greenish yellow around two deep circles of purple, made his gut tightened. "What is this?" he asked, studying the peculiar traces.

"I'm clumsy." Her voice hitched, revealing the falsehood of her words.

"Lying is a sin." He looked closer, turning her wrist gently. "These are..." Jesse knew the look of one after being manhandled, had sported a few similar marks himself once upon a time. "Catherine, who did this to you?" She clamped down on her bottom lip tighter, showing she had no intention of answering him.

"Daniel would never..." Suddenly Jesse knew. Letting go of her hand, he marched to where he'd been sitting before she came upon him and collected his hat.

"Where are you going?"

"To have a word with Irvin Miller."

"Jesse, no!"

"*Nee?*" He shot back. "I know Daniel wouldn't lay hands on you this way. Does he know of this?"

"*Nee*, and he doesn't need to. You promised you wouldn't."

Was she serious? He had been young when he learned the difference between obedience and pain and that not all fathers were the same. The rod was not used equally on all kinner. "Daniel will have his hide, if there's any left on him."

Gripping Jesse's shirt, Catherine made a bold attempt to stop him. "You can't do that. It's not our way. Have you forgotten that?"

"Neither is that," he motioned towards her hand. "I've forgotten nothing, Catherine." In a moment of clarity he let out a raging breath. What did she think he would do after finding out someone had mishandled her? "But I've yet to join the church."

"Yet?" Her question held a hint of chastisement in blue eyes that matched a mountain lake.

"I'm staying and taking baptismal classes. I'm ready to start a family...here."

"I'm happy for you, and I'm certain your *mamm* will be glad to hear of it. Then you understand why we must let this go. You don't need to draw eyes on you right now. I'm fine. More than fine, really." She paused, looking about as if words were painted on trees and stones. Did she realize she was still clinging to his arm? "I don't need everyone to know."

That was it, the root of her concerns. Catherine worked harder than most, tiptoeing down the center of the straight and narrow.

Touching her cheek, Jesse sighed. He knew how it felt, being the center of attention. Like him, Catherine wanted a simple life and to live it without shadows of mistakes hovering over it.

"I can not just do nothing Catherine. He laid hands on you. Do you understand?"

SHE SHOULDN'T HAVE LIKED the look of the devil dancing in his dark eyes, but she did. To know someone besides her own father cared this much sent all kinds of new emotions surging through her. However, she would not uphold sin or violence. She was Daniel Raber's daughter and would not shame his name any further.

"*Nee*. I don't understand. I'm Catherine, the short haired girl with the strange accent you teased into tears. You're Jesse, the cruel boy who said mean things and ran away from home. This is none of your concern.

"Is it not? Irvin is not right for you, and you know it." He brushed her cheek with the back of his hand.

"He said the same of you," she told him.

"I have never been interested in another woman," he admitted.

"What about Megan? I heard what Irvin said. That she named a child after you. You say you are home to stay, that you will join our church. What about them?"

"It's not like that. I helped her one night when she found herself needing it. There is nothing going on between us, nor has there ever been."

"She is very beautiful," she lowered her gaze.

"And yet, you are the one that makes me trip over my tongue. Go figure." He laughed, caressing her cheek. Oh how he loved her. "The truth is I crossed paths with her long ago. She was in the family way, and I soon learned she was ready to give birth. I helped her to the hospital. She was just a child and all alone. I'm glad I was there. They could have both lost their lives. She makes more of it than it was. I hadn't seen her since that night, until you saw me in town at the drugstore. She is just grateful, Cat, that's all. She wanted me to meet her daughter, the baby that was saved that night. I don't date *Englischers*." He grinned. "I have never wanted to live any other way. I may have been forgotten by some, pushed out by others, but...I've never let go of my faith."

He was telling the truth. Those eyes could charm and disarm with one look, but they were honest. He quirked a grin. It was crazy what he did to her system. A roller coaster of feelings, all crashing into one another.

"I guess I did jump to conclusions. I just don't know you."

"You are making it awful hard to get to know me by holding on to what a fool I was as a boy. There is so much I missed too," he lowered his head. "So we can get to know each other all over again."

Cathereine took a shuddering breath. "You want to get to know me?" *Like, get to know me, get to know me?*

"Why else would I be here?" Six little words, a mountainous impact.

"You say these things, but…we don't even like each other."

"Don't be afraid to have a change of heart."

"I'm not afraid." She shot him a cold stare.

"I'm glad to hear it." He laughed, seconds before his lips landed on hers. Catherine hadn't prepared for spontaneity. She should have fought it, just as she had the first time someone tried stealing what was hers, but she couldn't. Jesse's lips invading hers was like everything Catherine imagined a first kiss to be. She really should protest. Jesse Plank was kissing her! Instead, Catherine melted into his embrace and didn't think at all.

"You grew up, and so did I," he whispered breathlessly. Stunned, that's what she was. She, Catherine Raber, had kissed her childhood nemeses and wanted to do it again. Lips swollen, she inhaled a sharp breath.

"I have wanted to do that for longer than you could ever know."

That wasn't just an accident?" He laughed at her innocent response.

"I didn't trip into you, and our lips just happened to align, Cat." He laughed again, cradling her cheek.

Still dazed and confused, she remained in his arms, staring up at her reflection in eyes dark with affection. "I thought you were just trying to shut me up," she admitted with naivety. "Stop laughing," she said, but found herself laughing too.

He leaned down again, stopping just a breath away. "Let me go at it another way." His lips barely brushed hers, sending a hope through her she had never anticipated.

"*Daed* will not be happy about this," she muttered back as she let his lips fall on hers again. If there was a rule she didn't know about concerning the number of kisses one should have in a single moment, she was sure she was breaking it. They broke apart when a thunderous sound came plundering through the trees.

"CATHERINE! Jesse! Please tell me the boys are with you." M.J. interrupted.

CHAPTER 19

*a*t the sight of her soaked dress and fallen hair, *Daed's* eyes narrowed as he studied her disarray before turning to Jesse with an equal disappointment. They were both drenched, out of breath, and looking as guilty as two people could get.

"I fell into the creek," Catherine quickly explained, working a few damp strands under her misshapen *kapp*.

"I tried helping, and it cost me a clean shirt," Jesse added, making light of the blooming intimacy they just shared.

"We'll deal with that later. My *sohns* are missing."

Catherine had seen that look before on her father's face and instantly felt the severity of the situation.

"We will find them," Jesse said, stepping forward and placing a hand on his shoulder.

As night drew closer, more than three dozen buggies filled the Raber driveway. Everyone wanted to see the boys home safely, coming to aid in the growing search. Catherine had kept coffee flowing to those who needed it, but as the night went deeper, she feared the fate of her young *bruders* was not a good one.

Standing on the porch, she watched as lamps, flashlights, and headlamps flickered like July fireflies over the fields and into the tree lines. Inside, Aenti Edith had started praying again. A soft snore from another room told her Hazel Fisher had fallen asleep again. The local baker struggled with the late hour more than most since she started her daily baking at three a.m.

"Oh, my sweet boys," *Mamm* covered her face in her hands to cry more tears. Millie Troyer, their nearest neighbor and *mamm's* dearest friend, went to her.

"Huck yerst ahna," Millie said, helping *Mamm* into a chair. She'd not ask *Mamm* to go rest. Not with the unknowing.

Catherine swatted a mayfly drawn in by the June night air and cascade of lighted lamps along the porch railing. If only she had been home, helping watch over them instead of down by the creek with Jesse, her *bruders* would be safe. She felt useless waiting with the other women while Henry and Bryan were out there alone.

Seeing another shadow emerge from the barn, Catherine strolled towards Jesse's silhouette. Surely he'd know if they had found any sign of Henry and Bryan.

"We checked all the way to the Troyers." He shook his head, revealing there was nothing of her *bruders* seen there. "Aiden, M.J., and Rosemary are going back down to look over the creek."

"I want to help, too." Jesse offered her his flashlight and clicked on his headlamp.

"We will find them," he added.

"Henry is smart, but he likes to test things. Oh, Jesse, what if…" He took her hand, gave it a slight squeeze in the shadows of darkness.

"Bryan is smart too. We *will* find them. You have to have faith that *Gott* is with us and them."

His optimism was stoic. Catherine never had that glass-half-full approach to life. She believed if a person wanted a full cup, they had to pour it for themselves. Jesse was right. She needed to have faith because there were no certainties in life.

Catherine whispered a silent prayer, and when she opened her eyes again, she noted Jesse had been doing the same. He truly was nothing like the boy who ran out of Miller's Creek all those years ago.

"We've searched everywhere," Jesse said as if he, too, was struggling to think they would find them soon.

Catherine tried to think. Henry was fond of the old shed, but that had been fully combed over. Bryan liked the hayloft, and it, too, had been searched. There was the creek, but if they had been there, they would have heard them.

"They don't stay within the boundaries." Jesse looked north then west, his eyes searching through the darkness as if capable of seeing what was concealed within its veil.

"What do you mean?" Catherine cocked her head to one side.

"If you tell them not to go outside without a coat, they do. Tell them not to dirty their best trousers, they…"

"They'd roll around in the mud." Catherine studied the lay of the land. "They would not be where we would expect them."

"Exactly. Where is the one place they know they are never permitted to go to?"

Catherine's eyes immediately shot to the far northern parcel and the forbidden meadow just beyond. It was a small tract of land between their farm and the Troyers filled with old rotting logs, limbs, and uncut grasses. "There," she pointed. "Since we were little, it's been off-limits. There was once an old house there. *Daed* says it's not safe and made each of us promise never to wander there. They know better."

"Not all young boys follow the rules," he shrugged. "*Komm.*" He urged her towards the northern pasture gate.

Catherine followed blindly, not sure Jesse understood how firm *Daed* had been about the old meadow, but sure enough, as they crested the hill under a rising half-moon, the sound of a small voice penetrated the evening air. "Jesse."

"I hear them. Watch your step," Jesse said with a sense of urgency and helped her weave around round stones and old wood rotted into decaying piles.

Catherine had a faint memory of the meadow from when she was nine. She weaved her light back and forth, noting the vast number of young saplings now dotting the small lot and the old oak she thought to be tall was now split in two by a bolt of lightning at some point in time.

"Did you two hear that?" Sam Lewis appeared to their left, a flashlight in hand. He had darker hair and eyes than his *bruder's*, but his deep voice and accent made him easy to recognize. More rustling followed, and soon M.J. and Aiden appeared too.

"Is that them?" M.J. and Aiden appeared from their left.

"I think so." Catherine reached out for her younger sister and clutched her hand into M.J.'s

"Watch your step," Jesse warned everyone. "Catherine said there was once an old house here. We can't know what's underfoot."

"Of all the places." M.J.'s breath was labored, and her grip tightened as they made their way over long boards and composted logs.

"The sun should rise soon enough," Sam informed them. "Henry! Bryan!" Sam called out, and soon the frantic cries of two small boys called back. Catherine rushed over a twisted log as her feet landed on something weak.

"Shine your lights here," Jesse ordered.

The earth sank here, and it was easy to see Jesse on his knees looking downward.

"What is it?" M.J. asked as she struggled to reach them.

"I see them!"

Catherine gasped at Jesse's words, and whispered an immediate thank you for *Gott* leading them here.

"You two hurt?" Jesse called down into the darkness.

"He won't stop stepping on my hands," Bryan fussed, sending a flood of relief through everyone.

"Oh, Bryan," Catherine stepped forward, blinking back tears of joy. "Don't move, okay?"

"It's dark, and we can't move in the dark, Cat," Henry answered, adding further relief to her panicky heart.

"They are right there," Catherine turned to tell M.J.. Her younger sister fell on her knees and looked for herself.

"Can we reach them?" she asked, inspecting the hole they'd somehow fallen in.

"I'll have to go down and fetch them. Looks like old lumber was tossed in, but we can't know how sturdy it is," Jesse said, shining his light around to anticipate the best approach.

"Stay to the left here," Sam suggested. He too was belly flat on the ground, inspecting the safety of a rescue. "Looks sturdier on this side, and it should keep things from falling."

Catherine appreciated Sam's help, but knowing how unstable it was sent a fresh panic through her. M.J. grasped her hands. She too knew how serious the trouble the two had gotten themselves into this time was.

"Here." Aiden dropped to the ground. "I'll hold onto you, in case."

Jesse looked up at Catherine. "Hold your light on my footing," he told her before turning to slide his first foot over the blunt edge.

The earth may swallow them all whole.

"I'm *komm*'n down a little. I want you both to grab hold of me when you can and slowly climb up," Jesse instructed both boys. Catherine's breath held. Would Bryan, in his frightened state, even be able to follow directions?

She handled a flashlight, its shaky beams bouncing unsteadily in her trembling hands. M.J. clutched her arms as if she too was climbing out of the abyss. With deft movements, Jesse climbed down until only the top of his head remained ground level. They were all on their knees. Beside her, M.J. began praying, her tears pouring out in buckets. Catherine didn't miss Sam Lewis reaching over and giving her sister's hand a squeeze. It was a kindness, offering her comfort. Catherine maneuvered the flashlight to Jesse's next steps.

Aiden had one hand wrapped tightly around Jesse's collarless shirt. The mint green was already dry from being pulled into the creek. His long legs held steady against rickety rocks and earth that still formed an old well's ramparts.

"This is as far as I can *komm* without making matters worse. Let's go, you two, climb up." A few grunts and complaints later, both little dark heads emerged from the earth in a birth of freshly born stupidity and blessed safety.

Catherine latched onto Henry immediately as M.J. pulled Bryan into her bosom.

"I can't believe you two were up here," M.J. fussed as she wiped away tears, and they began inspecting them for injuries in beams of broken early morning light and tears of joy. Dirty, a couple scrapes band aid worthy, but no worse for wear.

Time. Everyone thought they had plenty of it. That a life of routine would never be shaken. But life shifted unexpectedly, and in a blink, life could disappear.

"Don't overthink it," his deep voice whispered near her. She hadn't even realized Jesse had climbed back out, too. His strong hand landed on her shoulder. "They are fine and maybe a bit wiser now." She sniffed back a few tears then hugged both *bruders* at once.

"Stop, Cat, we can't breathe," Henry fussed, earning a few laughs. Aiden swooped him up and gave him a slight tickle.

"Let's get you two back to Hannah," Aiden said. Jesse lifted

Bryan, a smaller version of the bigger one, and sat him on his shoulders.

"*Daed*'s going to be mad," Bryan muttered. "I lost my hat."

"Hats can be replaced," M.J. poked his side. "Little *bruders* cannot."

"But *Daed* just bought it," Bryan said.

"*Jah*, he is gonna be mad at you," Henry put in. "He said if you lose another one, he'd punish you for sure."

"He said if you brought another snake home, he'd punish you, too," Bryan countered. Seemed life and death situations had done nothing to lessen their quarrels.

"A snake?" So that's what caused two little boys to venture into unsafe territory? Catherine held her tongue. Whatever she had in mind to say would be nothing compared to how their parents would react.

They all watched Hannah scoop up both dirty boys and cry tears of relief. "Mothers and sons have a bond that near death adventures and mud-streaked faces elude," Jesse said in a low voice. Catherine shot him a look.

"They do." Was he thinking of his *mamm*? Would she someday have such a nearness to sons of her own? At Rosemary's urging, Catherine slipped into the house, but she felt Jesse's gaze on her all the way.

In the last 24 hours, Catherine had her fill of experiences. It started out full of terrifying moments and ended nearly the same, but it was that middle part, a kiss down by the creek, currently running through her mind as she helped serve fresh *kaffi* and watched Jesse explain to *Daed* and the bishop all the details around the boys' rescue. How Eli Plank didn't see what a fine man his *sohn* had grown into was beyond her. Because that was plain to see.

Catherine offered Jesse a cup of coffee and whispered, "You are as dirty as my *bruders*."

"Guess I could jump in the creek again," his low voice mocked, and she felt her face warm.

"You surprised me today."

He lifted a brow. "Which part? It has been an eventful day with you, Catherine." Could she dare tell him? Composing herself accordingly, Catherine lifted her shoulders and tried to appear unaffected.

"All of them," she replied. "You should know I don't like surprises." She focused on the crowd that was thinning, the attention two little mischief makers were getting, and not the man standing just behind her watching it all as the sun lifted over the horizon.

"*Jah*, but I do enjoy watching you receive them." It was hard to argue away how she felt right now. He had rescued her, twice, and then her brothers. As she watched him drink, Catherine studied the man and began mentally listing his finer qualities. He would make a good father. Fun, where she was serious, stern, where she was weak hearted. The very thought caused her heart to beat a little faster.

CHAPTER 20

"*B*ut, I've been working with you at the mill since I was nine!" Catherine didn't believe in raising her voice, but as *Daed* delivered his harshest punishment to her, she found no way to timid her tone. It had been Henry and Bryan who'd gotten themselves in harm's way, yet it was Catherine paying for it.

"Your duty is to your family…not the mill," *Daed* said sternly. "You will help your *mamm* at home. Help keep those two stay out of trouble." Where had gone the father who took her for milkshakes to make her smile? Where had the man who owned her heart left his understanding and fairness?

"It's not my fault they went to the well in search of snakes." She tapped down the need to yell, but spoke loud enough to make an impact.

"School is out, and instead of swimming, you will be here watching over them," he said, ignoring her defenses. Was he punishing her for not being home when her *bruders* ran off, or for falling in the creek?

"You talk as if I can't see over my own *kinner*," *Mamm* said. "It's as much my fault as any. I am their mother."

"It was no one person's fault," he softened. "But Edith still feels poorly and needs you. You can't take those two over there right now and bring sickness back into the house. Edith is older, and I know how you worry about her health." He turned to Catherine again, resuming his previous scowl. "Catherine can handle Henry and Bryan well enough."

"You're not being fair. You know you can't do it all yourself. You need me to tally the tickets and keep the books. Who's gonna check phone messages and fill out lumber orders?" Catherine continued to plead with him. It wasn't just her that was affected, but their livelihood.

"You managed well enough without me for a spell. I figure I can do the same. Besides, no sense in you living a life centered around a dirty old mill." He lifted a finger when her mouth opened to protest again. "You will do as you are told."

Catherine held back the sob, refusing to let him see her tears. Her life was the mill. Her everyday life revolved around it. Without another word, her father left, leaving Catherine and her *mamm* staring after him.

"He's punishing me because of Jesse." Catherine fell into the kitchen chair and burst into tears.

"He isn't punishing you; he trusts you. Henry and Bryan gave him such a scare he just doesn't know how to handle the fear that ran through him. Don't you remember? I know you do. He once fretted terribly over you and your *schwestern*." Hannah cradled her cheeks. "That day we learned you never made it to school, that you were taken," Hannah sucked in a breath. "I never saw a man so scared for another as he was that day. Never underestimate your father's love for you. It's endless, Catherine."

"He should trust me." Catherine wiped her tears away with a length of her sleeve.

"Men can't handle fear; they think themselves invincible

and capable of stopping bad things from happening." Catherine nodded. Had not Jesse eluded the same fear?

Catherine stood and peered out the window towards the barn where the lamplight glowed. She felt a hand touch her shoulder. "Stop fretting, my *lieb*. Jesse isn't going anywhere. I knew the moment he showed up he was home for good. Now help me load up all my quilting stuff to take with me to Edith's. It helps her to stay put in the bed and not think to cook for me," *Mamm* smiled. Today was going to be a long day.

The next morning Rosemary lazily worked the brush through her dark hair. "I saw you chasing Henry yesterday morning. What game was that?"

Catherine let out a weary breath. "No game. My *kapp* blew off, and he thought it fun to run off with it." She frowned. "Bryan tried swinging from the barn rafters too. He may be the quieter one, but trust me, sister, that one is just as determined to induce heart attacks as is Henry."

"Oh, I know it. I caught Henry poking a stick into one of the hives a couple days ago, but just two feet away stood Bryan holding a jar." Rosemary chuckled. "I do love my *bruders* but they are a test for the weak, for sure. They say it takes a village to raise up a child, and now we know why."

"M.J. never seems to have troubles with them." Catherine finished folding the last of the towels.

"M.J. teaches them half the stuff they do," Rosemary said. That was true enough. Martha Jane Raber did have a habit for testing limits.

Catherine half smiled at the memory. Her mind was on everything but the two brothers she was to keep an eye on.

"Is it so bad, I mean, staying here as opposed to working at the mill?"

"*Nee*, I actually have enjoyed the time with them, heart attacks and all, but *Daed* shouldn't have done it."

"Don't be upset, I know the mill is your thing, but..." Rosemary paused and touched Catherine's arm with a tender touch,

Catherine didn't like the look of concern on her sister's face.

"*Daed* asked me to come over tomorrow morning to answer phones for a few hours."

Catherine's heart felt the sting of Rosemary's words. She'd not blame Rosemary. She was the most wonderful person Catherine knew. Harnessing her disappointment, Catherine knew Rosemary would rather be on the farm, working with her bees and creating new cheese flavors to sell at the Amish Market. Everyone was making sacrifices. Even Rosemary.

"He surely could use the help. But what about your cheese order for this week? I haven't helped in years. I wouldn't even know where to start." The right thing to do, under the circumstances their father had put them in, was to help Rosemary in turn, but the thought of making cheese for hours had her breakfast refusing to digest.

"I'm sure it's just for the morning. I can see to it when I get home, but I will need you to strain and store whatever M.J. collects." Rosemary worked her damp brown hair into a knot and pinned it securely into place.

"That I can do," Catherine agreed. "Maybe you can show me how to make the simple recipes once more." Rosemary brow lifted. "Don't look at me that way. I can do it."

"Nee, I know you can. I'm just sorry about this. I know you love your work." Sincerity showed in her sister's brown eyes.

"He's punishing me." Catherine couldn't pretend to be content with their father's decision.

"It's not your fault the boys get into mischief regularly." Rosemary slipped her *kapp* over the wide bun.

"He thinks there is something going on between me and Jesse," Catherine admitted in the privacy of the two of them.

"Of course there is." Rosemary stood and winked. "We all know, so best not to deny it. It will only make it harder for you to accept what your heart already has."

Catherine couldn't. She was attracted to Jesse and if she was being honest, falling for him head over heels. "I wish I could," Catherine admitted.

For the following days, Rosemary continued to walk the well-trodden path to the mill each morning. Catherine did her best to make cheese for the market in her place, but her first attempts were a total loss. Catherine blamed two eager brothers who made it a chore to stay on task.

Thankfully Aenti Edith began feeling well again, her strength returning. Once *Mamm* was home, Catherine no longer had Henry and Bryan underfoot all day and worked harder not to spoil any more milk. It took over a week and Rosemary's calm instructions, but Catherine found her own rhythm and found the process of making cheese strangely satisfying. The quiet house over the racket at the mill, along with the leisure of time, gave a person a lot of time to think about what was important. To think about how one could be a better version of one's self. And to think about Jesse Plank. She was doing a lot of that.

She missed him. God help her, she did. He was the last

man she wanted to imagine herself with. The last man she wanted to give her heart to. But the very one she knew who had always stolen her thoughts.

Yesterday afternoon he'd found her in the garden, pulling weeds trying to smother out healthy bean plants. Their visit was short-lived, but he made a joke about his love for potatoes, his dislike for parsnips, and popped a small jelly bean tomato into his mouth, and smiled. It was casual talk, but she reveled in it.

He ate supper at the table each evening, but she barely dared a glance his way so as not to upset her *daed*. Jesse didn't care, though; his eyes found her often and plenty. They hadn't spoken of that kiss, the one that had closed gaps the years had formed, but as she climbed up the ladder into the loft of the barn where he slept, it was fresh in her thoughts.

Catherine made quick work of stripping the bed and putting down fresh linens. Rosemary once mentioned a box, treasures from his travels they both guessed. Funny how all her life she had been told a man who wandered had no home. He jumped fences, and his faith was weak. Jesse wasn't any of those things she was discovering. There was a reason he left Millers Creek. If only she knew what that was. Had Eli pushed his only child away intentionally? It was Jesse's secret, was it not? Catherine had her own hidden past too. Perhaps neither of them would ever know the roads they traveled to get to where they were now.

Jesse's Bible sat on a crate nearby. Tiptoeing gently over the aged, wooden loft floors, hoping Henry and Bryan wouldn't notice and follow, she lifted the Bible into her hands. The old black leather was worn, and inside his name was scribed in the delicate hand. Running her finger over a worn postcard tucked between pages from somewhere called Rexford, Montana, she studied the picture. It was a long prairie hemmed in by glorious mountains. It was beautiful, much more so than Miller's Creek, Kentucky.

Upon further invasion of Jesse's privacy, she found the dried flower, lifted it tenderly and turned it between two fingers. Had it been a gift from some sweetheart or a family member? She suddenly wanted to know what made a man hold on to it so long.

"Are you looking for something in particular?"

Catherine turned to find Jesse standing atop the landing. Her face went shamefully hot. Jesse lifted a brow, taking one corner of his mouth with it to form a questionable grin. If he was angry she was going through his private things, it didn't show.

"I wouldn't have thought you to be someone who kept flowers in a Bible."

Walking to her, Jesse took up the Bible and delicate flower. "I appreciate *Gott*'s simple beauties." He tucked the flower back in place and set the Bible on the bed. Both were obviously precious to him, and that made her wonder if the flower held some sort of memory. Had he fallen in love out there, before being called home? Did the flower represent some perfect moment he never wanted to forget?

"*Mamm* does that," Catherine informed him. "She dries and saves flowers to put in a devotional book she has. I think *Daed* must have given her most of them."

That's when Catherine noticed the long rip in the side of Jesse's shirt. "Are you alright?"

"I'm fine. Just got too close to the edger. Thankfully it has two shutoffs," he said, fetching a clean shirt from a nearby nail hanging on a two-by-four.

"What kind of flower is it?" Catherine turned when he lifted his ripped shirt over his head to replace it with a new shirt.

"I'm done, you can turn around now." She did and found her head dizzy, if not by the spinning, than by the man.

"Jasmine," Jesse added with a slow grin.

Jasmine had always been Catherine's favorite scent. Though it wasn't proper to wear fancy lotions and perfumes, she'd fallen in love with the scent long ago. She made sure to keep a bottle in her dresser drawer at all times. Adding a light spritz to her pillow was not forbidden.

"It took a while to find it."

"You looked for it," her voice pitched slightly.

"For a long time." His voice drew deep as he moved closer. "I happen to be fond of the scent. Always have been." He brushed the back of his hand over her cheek.

"How long?" Her voice quivered. There was no way he knew Jasmine was her favorite scent. "How long have you had that flower? How long did you look for it? How long? Where in Rexford, Montana?"

"I've had that," he pointed towards the Bible, "for six years now." His gaze grew intense. "I was in Rexford for about three. That sky, that blue," he looked into her eyes, "reminded me of home. Just like the Jasmine reminded me of…" he paused, not telling her what they reminded him of exactly.

"Of what? Is this why you returned?"

"I came home because *Daed* was hurt. They need me, and we need to fix what's broken. I came home for forgiveness too," he said simply. "*Mamm* and I have spoken, but *Daed*," he placed his straw hat back over his unruly dark hair. "Well, some things don't change no matter how much time passes."

"I'm sorry." Catherine truly was. No matter how upset she was with her own father currently, Jesse and Eli had been at odds since she knew them.

"I didn't grow up like you, Catherine. You are blessed to have Hannah, Daniel, your sisters, and even those two troublemakers."

"I am blessed to have them, but, Jesse," she paused, gave her bottom lip a tug as she calculated her next words. "Don't give up trying to mend what's broken there."

"You should know I don't give up easily once my mind's made up." His eyes narrowed as he gazed at her, and the unspoken words behind them sent butterflies fluttering in her belly.

"I should apologize for touching your private things. It was wrong of me, and…"

"I have nothing to hide from you, Catherine." It was permission to enter his world, breathe his air, and he knew it was a gift she hadn't expected.

"I've missed seeing you at the mill. I'm sorry too," he added.

"You shouldn't have kissed me," she said. She would have been fine if not for that kiss.

"You did return that kiss, as I recall," he quirked a grin.

"Well…I…I forgot, and you did surprise me," she blurted out.

"Forgot what?" He placed a hand on her upper arm.

"I forgot to hate you. My memory has returned. I let you get to me years ago, when I should have just ignored you, and you're doing it again." Jesse couldn't help but laugh.

Jesse took a step back. "Then go. No one is making you do anything you don't want to do, Catherine, and I give you my word that I'll not…surprise you again until you forget you don't like me." Tipping his hat to her, Jesse descended back down the ladder, leaving Catherine alone in the barn loft trying to decide if putting the past behind them would mean more kissing.

CHAPTER 21

neeling in his mother's garden, Jesse thought of Catherine. The flicker of surprise that came over her face when he told her about the dried sprig of Jasmine. Did she know the truth behind the flowery scent? Would he dare reveal his love for her so soon?

There was much to consider before confessions were made, he measured. Until he joined the church, he couldn't ask her to court him, and Jesse didn't want Bishop Schwartz to get the wrong impression of Jesse's faith. It was hard to outgrow people's assumptions, and he still wasn't sure if Daniel would accept him. When Daniel requested Jesse stop eating his meals in a dirty barn, Jesse took it as a sign that he might find favor in Jesse. Then again, everyone knew the reasoning for keeping Catherine at home instead of working at the mill was his doing and not Henry and Bryan's latest troubles.

"Edith says you only have a couple more baptismal lessons," *Mamm* said, hunkered down in a row full of zinnias. She always loved the simple flowers with vibrant colors.

"It wonders me if he didn't add a few lessons in there for me especially," Jesse jested. Over the last couple of weeks Jesse had answered all of her questions. Jesse obliged her and, in turn, learned a lot about how Millers Creek had shrunk and grown in his time away. It was when she queried him about Catherine, Jesse finally relaxed under his father's sharp gaze from the living room window.

"Perhaps he too has seen you have eyes for Daniel's daughter," *Mamm* lifted a brow.

"It's a wonder she speaks to me at all. It's my fault she isn't at the mill each day. If I didn't need the money, I would walk away."

"Don't say that. If you care for her, don't leave her."

"*Like I did you*," Jesse wanted to say. "I left the first time because *Daed* made me. You know that." She did. If anyone knew, *Mamm* did. "I don't know how to walk away from her."

"You have plans to marry her then, *jah*?" Sara Plank still possessed a third eye, reading his mind like a book.

"I do, but it will take some time. I don't exactly have anything to offer her. It will take a couple years to grow my pocket, and that's if she'll have me."

"If you didn't insist on sending us money all the time, you would have more." His *mamm* returned to deadheading dried flower blooms.

"You're my *mamm*. How can I not see you taken care of?"

"You are a *goot sohn*. I always knew you would be a *goot* man too." The words warmed his heart. "Tomorrow, you will come pick me up. I have a check-up with my *doktor*, and we need to make a stop for you." Jesse wanted the opportunity to meet her doctors and learn more about what she needed. He suspected his father might have a say in that, but he would do as *Mamm* asked, no matter.

"I don't need to go anywhere, but I'd be glad to take you for your check-up."

"You must go to the bank in town."

Jesse stopped pulling weeds crowding out cucumber vines and gave her a perplexed look.

"I have a confession to make," Sara said grinning, her eyes showing a glint of joy.

"Confession?" Jesse chuckled. His mother was the most decent person he knew. She was the epitome of a devoted *fraa*.

"You know your father ordered me to burn everything you sent. All those beautiful postcards from different places, letters you had written, and the money you sent." Only Eli Plank would burn money to prove a point. Jesse simply shook his head and leaned heavily on the gardening hoe.

"Paul told me of it, but that's why he saw my letters put in your hand himself, when *Daed* was away. Please tell me you didn't burn all of it." His mother smiled cunningly.

"Paul did come. He would sneak here when your *Daed* was working at the mill." She smiled. "Perhaps you learned to keep so many secrets from me because I knew where you were, and my heart worried less reading your letters." She swallowed and looked towards the house. "I may have not done what was asked of me, but I trust that *Gott* understands the reasons behind my falling short as a dutiful *fraa*." Under dark lashes she looked up to him with a slyness Jesse didn't know she possessed.

His poor innocent mother fretted too easily. "You are not one to disobey orders."

"I have done more than read your letters." She wiped a bit of perspiration from her brow and reached into her apron pocket, pulling out a narrow strip of paper and offering it to him.

"What's this?" Jesse let the hoe fall to the ground and took the paper reading Community Trust Bank in blue across the top.

"All your hard earned money." Jesse's mouth fell open as he looked down at the gift he called *mamm*. A fragile sort who didn't defy rules.

"I did little to help you or make your life easier," she said, shaking her head. "For either of us really, and it's only a matter of time before your *Daed* insists you not be permitted to come see me, but for eight years, my *sohn* worked all over this country making a good living, *jah*? It's time he gets to use it."

A single tear slipped down Jesse's cheek. Eight years of wages tucked away for safekeeping. For today. *Mamm* had given him a future, and the timing was well played. Eli Plank had been patient long enough. As soon as the rest of his fences were repaired, his gardens planted, and the barn back in shape so that even a tender breeze couldn't knock it over, Jesse would not be welcomed there again.

"He won't like this," Jesse motioned towards the house. "I can't believe he hasn't come out and run me off yet."

"He has a heart, Jesse. He just doesn't know how to use it." Jesse looked over to her in the honest words, but she was focused on dead flowers. "Eli had a hard upbringing, and his parents weren't the most kind."

"I never knew them," Jesse said.

"*Nee*, they were gone before you came into this world." She paused to glance towards the house. "I suppose that was harder for him, losing them. He has lost many close to him, including a *sohn*."

"He told me to go," Jesse reminded her flatly.

"I reckon it is his stubbornness you have after all. You didn't have to leave Millers Creek, though my heart says you leaving helped you see things from different angles. Your leaving gave him a reason to hold onto his anger. It will take time. All things do. But…" she turned to him, "he will. My Eli will see *Gott* returned you to us so we could be a family again. Eli will see his mistake in it all, and maybe one day he may even ask for your forgiveness."

Jesse wanted that too, but he wouldn't hold his breath. Eli Plank was by all measures of stubbornness the most devout.

"This money was meant for you both, to see you had the things you needed."

"I have everything I need. The Lord has always provided me with more than enough, but you... you have a life to begin." She wrapped both willowy arms around him and smiled. "And you need to start soon because Hannah and I really do want *grosskinner*."

HANNAH RABER WAS AN EXCELLENT COOK, but Jesse already knew that by the dozen of meals she made for him. So instead of focusing on the meatloaf or his second helping of blackberry cobbler that could make a man feel he had earned his keep, he focused on the woman across the table. She ate like a bird.

M.J. rattled on about the comings and goings at the market, but Jesse paid her little mind. It was a set of blue eyes stealing glances his way that made him ready to set in motion all the proper things required to reach his long awaited goal. Marrying Catherine Raber. It was hard to keep a thing such as the gift his mother had given him today to himself, but timing was everything. When she dared another look at him, Jesse captured it and held her there.

"You don't need a saddle," Jesse jerked back to attention at Hannah's words. He leaned back in his chair and listened as Henry tried to convince Daniel that making a saddle for goats was feasible thinking. He liked the boys, mischievousness and all.

"Henry tried riding Princess Fiona again. I told him he was going to break his neck," Rosemary informed before standing to clear the table. Catherine lifted her barely touched plate and went to help her.

"He fell off three times." Bryan burst out laughing.

"You two best not be hurting my goats," M.J. scolded. "*Daed*, tell them. Tell them I get less milk when they act a fool with them."

"*Sohns*, there will be no more messing with those goats. I think pulling weeds for your *Mamm* all day tomorrow will keep you busy enough." Both boys grumbled.

"I could take them to Joshua and Edith's too," Hannah put in. "Joshua could use a hand in the barn." Daniel agreed, which earned more groans.

Jesse sat back, listening to the exchange of father and sons, watching the smooth rhythm of mother and daughters. If God blessed him with sons, Jesse would be more like Daniel, fewer trips to the woodshed for sure and certain. Hard work taught a man many lessons physical punishment never could, and they would be the better for it. If *dochdern* was God's plan, then he would be just as soft as the man at the head of the table too, he predicted.

He arrowed his gaze on his mark and contemplated his strategy. Catherine scraped plates as Rosemary began filling the sink. She moved with a rare poise, a quiet nature that had always intrigued him. Everything about her captivated him. Even the way her bare feet soundlessly moved across the old wooden floor. Like floating, yet rooted to everything around her. A strange and mysterious mix.

Tomorrow he would be finishing paperwork at the bank, and already Paul was drawing up plans for a house. If she only knew to what lengths he would go for her. Well, he thought, pulling his gaze away and standing, she soon would. He was putting all his faith in the hope she felt something for him, something that would grow and never stop growing. It would be terribly disappointing to live next door to Daniel Raber and those pesky goats, if not. The boy in him quieted. He was doubtful, and feeling as if he would never measure up.

"*Danke* for another wonderful meal, Hannah," Jesse offered. "I best call it an early night." Catherine glanced over her shoulder, floating him a weak smile. It was enough. It was enough for today. He smiled back before aiming for the barn.

The next morning, Jesse moaned when the stirring broke into his dream. If that pesky goat was trying to ruin the perfect dream, it had succeeded. He opened one eye, noted the frail stream of light piercing through the barn slats, and hurried to his feet. In all his years he had never overslept. Not even once. If he hadn't been plotting out his future like a lovesick boy, he might have fallen asleep faster. Tugging on his trousers, he grumbled then quickly slipped into his boots. Across the room, in the darkening shadows, he made out the white *kapp* rising up out of the floor. She balanced a tray in one hand, climbed the ladder with the other. Jesse reached for a shirt and began sliding into it when he realized it wasn't Hannah or Rosemary who usually delivered him a warm breakfast.

It was Catherine.

She had never attempted to bring him breakfast before. Walls were crashing down, and he couldn't stop smiling at the destruction of them.

"*Goot mariya!*" he called out quickly, tucking in his shirt and lifting his suspenders over his frame. *So now you're acting shy,* his mind chided. She advanced forward, oblivious to his inner scrutiny.

"Omelets and oatmeal," she greeted and moved to set the tray on the foot of the bed. "*Mamm* feared you might have become ill too. So many in the community have caught this stomach virus, and it keeps making its rounds."

"*Nee,* just overslept for the first time in my life," he sputtered out. In the light, he could see the faintest hint of rose on her cheeks. Now they were both blushing.

"I sprinkled cinnamon on your oatmeal. Hope you don't mind. Wasn't sure what you liked." She shrugged.

"*You* cooked? For me?"

"I cook," she grinned and turned from his stare. "In a house full of cooks, amazing cooks, I rarely get my turn at it, but now I get more than my share." Her face dropped into a sadness he felt responsible for.

"I'm sorry." She waved off the apology and wandered the room idly. Jesse knew she was brooding over not working at the mill.

"We used to play up here all the time. Share secrets, hide from *Mamm.*" Her smile was gradual, and he watched her with pointed interest.

"You were always a very close family." Jesse lifted the bowl of oatmeal, breathed in the sweet cinnamon aroma, and sampled it.

"They will always come first."

He didn't take offense. Jesse liked her stance on the topic. Something he might never know how to offer children of his own. Children he hoped and prayed were her own, too.

Giggles broke out below, along with begging bleats of goats ready to be milked. "Those two are helping M.J. this morning. It's her day off," Catherine shrugged adorably. "I think even the goats know when trouble is near."

Jesse laughed, but his heart was doing flips as she lingered, a shy look bashfully playing with her features. He didn't want to rush her. Whatever she had come to say, Jesse would give her all the time she needed to say it.

"Those two are worse than when Paul and Aiden and I were *kinner*." Jesse took a second bite of oatmeal. "Delicious."

"*Danke*," she nodded.

"I caught them yesterday racing goats in the back field. No saddle needed. Glad I stopped them before M.J. got home, or you might have two less siblings."

She laughed. "Rosemary still has a stake in it," Catherine added. "Though these days, Raber Cheese is what I'm doing. I think she hates that as much as I hate knowing she's keeping my books."

"I'm sure she does. Did you know Rosemary sings? I mean to the goats, the horses…"

"The bees," Catherine quickly added. "*Jah*. Rosemary loves to sing. Few know. Most people think she's shy, but she isn't."

She was guarded, Jesses observed, but over the last few weeks he and Rosemary had exchanged numerous words. She was not shy. "I like her bee suit." Jesse took another slow bite, savoring this time alone with her.

"She looks like a gigantic marshmallow. But singing, well,

singing means she's happy. Rosemary deserves happiness more than anyone I know." Jesse paused in chewing the warm cinnamon and brown sugar mixture and swallowed.

"We all deserve that," he reminded her.

"I should go before those two get into something on my watch." She moved towards the ladder and began to descend. "Oh, do you like tuna?"

Jesse lifted a brow. "I do."

"Good. I'm fixing lunch today. Of course I won't be delivering it, but…" she stopped, leaving him to wonder about her next words. Catherine wanted to feed him, and that was enough.

"You can run a business, cook, make cheese, though you don't eat it, and can manage those two wild *kinner* below. Any more talents you've been hiding?" He floated her a devilish smile.

"You have been gone a long time, Jesse Plank." Her smile was flirtatious, and she quickly disappeared under the loft floor as she made her way back down. He smiled and felt life was finally going as it should be before diving straight into his omelet.

CHAPTER 22

*M*inister Graber's voice had a way of reaching beyond the walls of the hosting family's large home. While he spoke of redemption, the gaining of grace, Jesse felt he'd paid a huge debt to stand before the community and recite the words of his baptism. He didn't need to look about to know *Mamm* would have tears. Jesse had traveled far to get to this moment. Submitting to God, accepting a life devoted to his faith.

After the service, Catherine took her place in line with the community to welcome him. When she reached out her hand and whispered, "Welcome," he held her gaze a little longer, squeezed her hand a little tighter.

"It was long overdue," he whispered back.

His father had been in the line of welcomers, but disappeared somewhere before making his way to welcome him. Jesse had hoped in front of so many, *Daed* would have seen the new man before him, too.

Through the fellowship meal, Eli Plank kept his head down and his back to Jesse. It was time to move past needing his father's approval. There was one father that mattered more, and Jesse was ready to prove to him he was worthy of the gifts he had been given.

Once everyone had their meal, Jesse watched Catherine help the other women clear tables. Near the side of the house, Irvin, too, was watching. Jesse locked eyes with him until Irvin looked away first. At sixteen, Catherine Raber had refused to accept a ride home with Jesse. That evening had changed everything. Today, he had no buggy. No horse, having only used the small single-seater Daniel allowed him to bring Henry and Bryan here today. But Jesse had two good feet, and the day was proving a fine late July day. With the newness of his fresh commitments before his community, he felt fairly confident Catherine wouldn't object to walking alongside him back to the Raber's farm.

"Jesse," Daniel approached. "Hannah and the *kinner* are heading over to the Troyers for a visit. I'd like you and I to talk."

Jesse looked beyond him as Catherine and M.J. disappeared through the front door of the local Bent and Dent owner's home. As much as a disappointment was leaving without asking Catherine to let him walk her home, he also knew Daniel would soon address the growing affection he saw between his eldest and Jesse.

"Let me go hitch up both buggies." Jesse headed to the barn. While he readied the family buggy for Hannah, and the single seater for Daniel, Jesse tried to anticipate the conversation awaiting him.

Voices lifted near the back of the house. The young folks were starting up an old familiar hymn. Paul and Aiden were in the center of the lot. Soon a game of basketball would begin with Paul having the advantage over most due to his great height. Jesse would much rather be challenging Paul at hoops, than riding with Daniel back to the farm, but how else could he voice his intentions if they didn't have this time alone?

Alone was not easily found under the shadow of the Raber family.

Jesse took up the reins and veered the buggy onto the main road. "I've misjudged you," Daniel said before pointing left. "Take the long way. It's a fine day."

"You're not the first to do so," Jesse replied and veered the high stepping gelding left onto Turkey Shoot Road. Jesse shifted uncomfortably in the seat as they veered down a narrow road most used as a shortcut.

"I reckon I owe you a thank you as well."

Jesse shot him a confused look. "You owe me nothing. You've given me work and a bed."

"True," Daniel said and crossed his arms. He was a large man, built from hard labor, and probably as solid as a rock despite flecks of gray sprinkling through his beard.

"Little gets past Hannah. My *fraa* really does have eyes in the back of her head." Daniel chuckled lightly before his face tightened once more. "I know about Irvin and those Lewis boys racing buggies. I already thanked Paul," he said before a cloud came over his features. "I wish Catherine had come to me with this, but…" He stiffened, a little hurt. The man truly loved his family with such a deep love Jesse could only look upon it in awe.

"She can't disappoint you. You *are* the most important man in her life," Jesse assured and watched Daniel's shoulders relax.

"Am I?" Daniel lifted a brow. It was a question Jesse too wished to have an answer to but didn't dare ask.

"If that is true, it won't always be such. A father must accept this. Loving them. Protecting them has been a privilege I've never taken lightly, and am very thankful for," Daniel conveyed.

"I understand." And Jesse did. Jesse had always suspected the Raber's were an odd bunch. From the time Daniel appeared with a *fraa* and *kinner* that seemed overly shy, he thought so. How many times had Catherine not followed the teacher's orders unless spoken in *Englisch*. Jesse and Paul had once tried to find out the truth, but no one seemed to notice how different the family was. That was why he kept a close eye on them. Fear or curiosity, he could no longer remember, but that second winter, it seemed he had been wrong. They weren't *Englischers* pretending to be Amish, but he had already fallen head over shoes for Catherine.

"There is another matter that has been weighing on me for some time now. From what I have learned, you have a habit of helping others."

"The bishop told you." Jesse looked straight ahead, his palms growing damp. He didn't like talking about that night, as he made himself believe for years he couldn't.

"I am glad I was there, no matter what it cost me," Jesse started before speaking of the evening his path crossed with Meagan.

As they pulled into the wide circle driveway, neither man attempted to move. "I was glad we made it to the hospital in time. The nurse told me it could have been worse." The nurse had also assumed Jesse was the young man responsible for Meagan's situation. That's why he left before knowing Meagan's family had been notified of the emergency delivery.

"Why did you not speak of this before?" Daniel scolded him. "Why let others think you stole a car?"

"I told *Daed* that night I wasn't anywhere near the sheriff's car, but he didn't believe me. He never believed me. He said he knew I did it because I was seen leaving the scene of the crime."

"Irvin," Daniel said, recalling that it was Irvin who showed up at the bishop's home after the sheriff arrived to point a finger at Jesse.

"I couldn't tell *Daed* or the bishop that I had helped bring a child into the world. I was sixteen, scared out of my wits, and knew I was in trouble for just being a part of it. She was scared, too, begging me never to tell anyone."

"So you ran away instead. Not very responsible either."

"*Nee*. I know that now." Both climbed down from the buggy and gathered at the post where Daniel tethered the horse. Jesse was sure Daniel was going to ask him to leave. No man wanted a wayward living under their roof.

"I couldn't tell the truth because I promised to keep it a secret, but I begged *Daed* to trust me. That I'd never steal anything, especially a car. *Daed* told me to go. He made me go," Jesse said and felt a pang of guilt for saying it. His father and Daniel worked together. They were friends. And friends stuck together.

"I can pack and be gone before they get home. I do appreciate you helping me when I got here, but I know you are *freinden* with *Daed*." Jesse moved towards the barn opening.

"I am *freinden* with everyone. Tell me, Jesse. Did you like living out there," Daniel nodded to the horizon.

"Some communities were wonderful places to visit. I met some good folks, a few not so *goot* too," he lifted a brow. "But it's hard to stay where you don't belong."

"I see," Daniel said. "Did you know I grew up in the city?"

And there it was. The Raber's were an odd lot. Jesse tried not to act surprised, but it was hard not to. Daniel was the perfect Amish father, husband, and man. "*Nee*, I did not."

"Few know this. My *Daed* was a strange man with big ideas. I was nine when we left Miller's Creek and our faith. The same age Catherine was when she moved here." Daniel had such a strong love for his children.

"I never liked living out there. It was loud and fast moving, but it is good to know that you never wandered beyond our faith during your travels."

No wonder his *kinner* loved him so much. Daniel was terribly understanding. "I did live in an apartment for a spell and worked on a ranch once for about two years. It was lonely and hard without the fellowship of others. Then again, I managed well enough."

"So, did you have an interest out there? Is there some sweet *maedel* awaiting your return?"

With this, Jesse felt the first trickle of nerves slowly cascade down his spine. "I'm ruined for any other. Afraid I gave my heart away long ago." Jesse's palm began to grow slick.

"You could reconnect. You have money, a job. A man your age should think about settling down and having a family."

"That's what I have been trying to do."

Daniel cocked his head to one side and grunted. Jesse didn't need to tell him to whom he was referring; a father knew. "I guess you're going to want my permission to court her now." Daniel said in a huff. Jesse closed his eyes and felt his chest give. Jesse couldn't change his past, but he could fight for his future. He opened his eyes and faced Daniel, confidence anew.

"That's not what I'm seeking." Daniel lifted a brow. "I love her, always have. I loved her the moment I saw her defend M.J. against a reckless boy. I loved her when I caught her giving her perfectly clean apron to Addie Troyer at a gathering, and she wore a dirty one so Addie felt better." Jesse laughed. "She hates looking unkempt worse than anything."

The corner of the big man's lips started to hike up slightly.

"I loved her when she outsmarted the teacher and when I caught her releasing grasshoppers we caught for fish bait as *kinner*." Jesse stepped closer. "I want your blessing to marry her."

"You're building the house before cutting the tree, *sohn*. There are steps to be taken."

"House is being built as we speak. Trees have already been cut." Jesse mentally enjoyed the flash of surprise that skidded across Daniel's face.

"It wonders me how a man living in my barn can afford to build a house. I must be paying you too much." Daniel folded his arms over his wide chest and looked at him, bemused.

"I have been sending money home to my parents for years. Since I left here," Jesse began to explain. Daniel looked doubtful. "He wouldn't accept it. He told *Mamm* to burn it actually." Jesse still couldn't believe what a gift his mother gave him, and the shock on Daniel's face confirmed it was indeed a gift.

"Sorry. I guess I never realized just how hard things had become in your household."

"My *Mamm* is an obedient *fraa*, but that was one order she didn't follow," Jesse grinned. "She put every dime in an account under my name." Jesse chuckled. "I'm not as poor as I thought," he shrugged. "And I got a good deal on a few acres from the Troyers, too. I have a steady job, I hope." Jesse paused, letting Daniel know he still held the cards. Then he gave Daniel a few more minutes. "Daniel, I have the house and the finances; now I just need the girl. My future is in your hands."

"You have my blessing to court my *dochter*. I cannot give you more than that today."

CHAPTER 23

*J*uly heat bore down on the small valley of Miller's Creek, but as Catherine leaned on the side of the house next to her sister Rosemary with her eyes closed, she was grateful that there was a breeze. They began counting as Henry and Bryan scampered off into the yard. Hide and seek was the dumbest game ever, but at least outdoors the air was more sufferable.

If these last few weeks had taught her anything since *Daed's* punishment of her not working at the mill, it was that being home all day carried as many obstacles to overcome as the mill did.

Mamm was busy seeing to her next quilt and new church trousers for the boys. M.J. accepted an extra day at the market to work since Aiden all of a sudden had to travel to Indiana and help a sick *onkel*. For some reason, M.J. thought ignoring him would make him change his mind. Catherine had learned that ignoring the right one only made you miss them more. *Daed* was at the table currently, going over the books, and Catherine was playing hide and seek with two little boys.

"Ready or not," Rosemary called out, snapping Catherine back to the present. "I'll go to the barn, Henry always hides there, but you should try around back. The last time we played, Bryan was behind the trees over there."

"I would think they would know by now to stop using the same hiding spots," Catherine said, unimpressed, before wandering right as Rosemary walked straight ahead. Rounding the house, past the yellow rosebush and fresh line of clothes drying in the sun, she veered left towards the goat pastures. A small grove of maple, walnut, and persimmon clustered together, giving perfect camouflage to boys with innocent imaginations. Since early this morning, when she watched Jesse ride away with Paul, she couldn't help but wonder what he was doing right now. Was he helping Sara in her garden or perhaps finally sitting on the porch with his *daed*, both finding forgiveness for the other in their hearts? She knew it plagued him, the need to close whatever gap widened between him and his father. Who would have guessed Eli was such a hardened *daed*? Forgiveness was their way. Even she had come to know holding on to some things just let evil eat away at one's soul.

Two bobwhites sprang into flight when she reached a patch of wild blackberries. She plucked a handful, tasted them, then gingerly slipped within the trees, mindful of her footing. Warm weather meant snakes, and nothing scared her more than the slithery beasts.

Moving deeper into the woods, she listened for Bryan. He never was much good at quiet. Something rustled, and she smiled. Just as she suspected, he couldn't stand still even for ten minutes to claim victory.

Tiptoeing playfully, she moved in on her mark, placing both hands on the bark of the tree before her. The massive oak separated her from the little trickster, and she readied to make her move. Springing into action, she jumped out. "Gotcha!"

He was leaning on the tree, a wide grin spread under dark

eyes partially hidden under the brim of his straw hat. "Jesse," Catherine said, jumping back. He was here, waiting, as if he knew she was coming.

"Bryan hid in the barn." He removed his hat and stood upright. "Rosemary kind of tricked you."

"Tricked me?"

"I wanted to see you," he admitted. She couldn't stop taking in his handsome features, the way his eyes somehow smiled when she was reflected in them. He looked happy, which made her happy.

"You've been gone a lot lately." She folded her hands over her middle, hoping not to sound too foolish.

"Had to help Paul and Aiden work on the house," he replied simply, then pulled his hand out from behind his back and presented her with a sweet collection of daisies. Her mouth opened, but words couldn't come out. "I've missed you, these days apart. Saw these in town and couldn't imagine not purchasing them."

"You *bought* me flowers?" She accepted them and fought back a sob. No one had ever given her flowers before.

"Well, ice cream seemed to be Daniel's thing," Jesse smirked. How did he know that? "Now, I know you hate surprises, but…" Her heart hammered in her chest as he looked down to her; that confident look that had once annoyed her only prompted her nerves to stand on end now.

"I have one, but you gotta come with me to get it," he said, tempting her.

"You got me something else?" She motioned to the gorgeous bouquet in her hands. It was enough. He was enough.

"Silly woman, *jah*. And before you start biting your lip and thinking too hard, Daniel has given me permission to take you to get it."

"He did?" her voice hitched in surprise. He had asked her

father first. "We can take *Mamm's* buggy and horse." She glanced towards the homestead and then back to him. She couldn't contain her excitement.

"No need. I have my own." When they reached his buggy, Catherine could only smile. Regret was such a stickler for visiting when not welcomed, but right then, Catherine regretted more than ever saying no to Jesse all those years ago. "I got a good deal on it from a man in Walnut Ridge. Seems he is about to have his second, so he no longer has use of a two-seater."

"And the horse?" Catherine was no animal lover, but she was gorgeous. Honey hued coat and snow capped mane. The horse nickered as Catherine gave her nose a rub and then tried to taste the daisies in her hand. "Those are mine," Catherine scolded, causing Jesse to laugh.

After a quick glance toward the house, Catherine noted *Mamm* waving from the large sitting room window. Their approval meant so much to her. At the barn, Rosemary stood with a hand shielding her eyes. Henry and Bryan stood at her side wearing cheesy grins.

"You planned all of this." It wasn't a question. Jesse offered her a hand up into the buggy.

"For longer than you think." He smiled and rounded the buggy. When he climbed in beside her, Catherine felt taller than she had ever felt before. This was a man a woman could feel stronger with, a man that proved change wasn't always a bad thing. That no matter what others thought, you could be a better version of yourself daily.

"Where are we going?" Jesse clicked his tongue, setting the evening into motion.

"I thought down by the creek, since it holds such sentimental value," he grinned over at her. *That kiss.* Her face began to flush.

"It was life changing," he returned, knowing her thoughts. "Just as the second one was." He reached over and took her hand. The warmth of his touch, the silent promise in his eyes, filled her heart with so much hope. He was the last person she thought God would send her, and yet, the only one meant for her. No doubts remained that he didn't feel as she felt. He didn't have to say the words for her to know. His affections and obvious devotions for her were honest.

"But then I thought about it and decided to show you my house instead."

"Your house!" She blurted out.

Less than five minutes later, Catherine got the first glimpse of the house he was referring to. It was a skeleton needing skin, but glorious in its raw state. Jesse parked the buggy up front in the beaten down pasture grasses and tethered the mare to a post framing the house.

"It has a ways to go, but I'm thinking of a wrap around porch," he said, helping Catherine from the buggy. "Let me get something real quick." He went to the back of the buggy, lifted the box attached, and pulled out a basket and blanket.

"You really did plan everything." She was impressed. More than impressed, she was over the moon happy. Her first time courting and going on a picnic had been a complete disaster. This one was already better by far.

"Not everything," he smirked and took up her hand again and led her to where the front door was presumed to go. "Step on that," he motioned to a block, and she used it to climb up onto the floor.

"How did you get the Troyer's to sell you part of their land?"

"I think your *mamm* had more of a hand in that, but I can be convincing when I need to be," Jesse chuckled.

"I agree." Catherine darted him a grin. "It's going to be big for just one man. Is this the kitchen area?" she asked and wandered into an area squared off to the right.

"I was thinking of the sitting room. Sunsets through large windows, and I can't wait to see it with snow." He set down the basket and began spreading out the blanket. A picnic, in his new home. A romantic gesture if ever there was one. "The kitchen is over here." He pulled her through another run of two by four walls. "Three windows over the sink," he demonstrated. "The sunrise will be glorious here," he said in a rare dreamy tone that had her picturing the sun rising from this very spot. His life had taken some turns, some she knew, some she didn't, but she knew enough to know what this house, this beginning of his own future, meant to him.

"I'm so happy for you, Jesse. You deserve this so much. Oh, look, you can see the mill from here."

"That was the plan." She turned to him for further explanation. "*Komm*, I brought tuna. Not as good as yours but thought it was perfect for the day." So he planned to stay working at the mill. That made Catherine feel just as full as seeing Jesse smile so much.

They ate sandwiches and chips and drank colas, while Jesse talked about life in the eight years they had been apart.

"I can't believe you saw a wolf up close," Catherine said, wide-eyed, clutching her dress tightly in her grasp. "I'm such a fraidy cat; I would have died."

"You jumped from a moving car once, so I recall you saying." Jesse shot her a smirk. She regretted letting that slip weeks ago. "There's nothing I would keep from you, if you asked. I hope you know that, Cat. You know the only secret I ever held, which wasn't much of a secret if I stuck around." He let out a breath, and Catherine reached out and touched his hand.

"I do understand. More than you know," she replied,

sensing he was hoping for the same trust in return. "Jesse," she set down her drink. "We can't live in the past."

"I know we can't."

"I know there are things...you're...curious about, but I made a promise never to speak of them."

"I understand and promise to never ask for anything more than you're willing to give." And again, Jesse Plank surprised her.

"But you want to?" She let the thought slip, but then his eyes softened.

"I cannot lie. When you moved here, you were different from the others. I think that's what made you stick out."

"That's putting it mildly," she snorted.

"I was stupid then." He turned his hand and wrapped it around hers still touching him. He needed that nearness and now, Catherine realized, she did too.

"Now I'm stupid for other reasons." She couldn't ignore the blush of his cheeks. "I want to know everything. Where you came from, what your life was like before. Why you jumped from a car." His voice deepened on that last curiosity. He seemed to want to say more but removed his straw hat instead, setting it to the side. "But it doesn't matter. The past *is* the past." It was, and seeing him like this, vulnerable and bearing all to her, made her think. Jesse, too, had a past, one of heartache that he carried like a yoke around his neck. If he could let go, look ahead and trust God, then so could she.

"I was born in Indiana," Catherine offered.

"My father used to beat me just because he could." He let her hand go and popped a chip in his mouth as if his confession equaled hers. Catherine swallowed. Many suspected such within the community but said little about it. Catherine tilted her head, studied his calm demeanor more closely. Then again, many thought Jesse had burned down barns and stolen cars too.

"It's your turn. Let's not get stuck on that," he urged.

Even while chewing he made her stupid heart flutter. "Well, *my* birth father was *Englisch*." Jesse's chewing slowed but he didn't seem alarmed as she would have expected. "He was a police detective." She gazed around at the makings of a home, one she knew he would fill with love. "I used to think he hung the moon. Saved the lost, protected the weak." She turned to him again, a tear sliding down her cheek at the memory of the man she couldn't even bring to vision anymore. "He wasn't. He was the opposite and did horrible things for money. He was killed because of it."

"I'm sorry. I didn't know."

"No one but Joshua and Edith do. And no one can, Jesse. This is our family's secret, one that our very lives depend on being kept a secret." She was trusting Jesse Plank with her family's most important secret. She wouldn't tell him she loved him first. She had her priorities, but if that wasn't love without proclaiming the words, Catherine didn't know what was.

"Lives depend on? Cat, is your mother in some sort of trouble?"

"*Nee*, Rosemary." She lowered her head.

"Rosemary?" Jesse blurted out in surprise.

"Well, all of us really, but Rosemary saw the man who killed him. We were put in the witness protection, and the F.B.I hurried us away just hours after it happened." She would never forget those long moments, those three days in hotel rooms, not knowing if danger would find them. Thank God M.J. was too young to remember it all now.

"This sounds like a novel. So is that why you came here? To hide from this man?"

"*Jah*, and he was arrested." She watched his body relax at that, but he still hadn't budged. "He actually found us here, with Daniel, and thought I was Rosemary." She shuttered to repeat the moments of her abduction. "Remember that day you teased me for having short hair?"

"Cat, I was only teasing. I thought we put that behind us." She watched the hurt skid across his face, regretting those days.

"*Nee*, I mean that day I was so upset I ran off from school. The man found me, pretended to be a cop, and took off with me." Jesse's jaw clenched. Catherine loved seeing that protective part of him surface. Like her *daed*, she felt he too would have acted and seen her safe that day.

"I don't know where we were going, but when I realized he wasn't who he said he was, I jumped. I opened the car door and just flung myself out. I didn't care if I was run over or broken to pieces; I just had to get away. I ran up the road. We weren't far from the mill, and I hid just above the saw mill in the rafters. After a while, the sheriff and Daniel and others came. I watched the killer sneak around, and I was so afraid to call out, fearing he would find me. Then everyone started going through the woods, looking for me." Her breath grew more rapid, reliving that day. "But Daniel and a deputy stayed behind, in case I showed up. The killer shot at the deputy, and Daniel saw me."

She turned to Jesse again, tears blinding her view of him. "He saved me, Jesse. He had no gun or anything. Just a short board and no fear for his own life, and knocked the killer out cold. He marched straight to me. I fell straight into his arms."

Tears couldn't be stopped now even if she tried. "That day, well…he was my *daed*. Daniel is my *daed*," she corrected. "And he did that for me. I can never love anyone as I do him."

"It's okay." He wiped her face free of tears and kissed her forehead. "I knew there was more to you. Now I know why. Why he loves you all so much and why it's so hard for you all to let go." He did get it. "I promise never to share your secret and am honored you shared it with me. You have no idea what that means for me, for us." Oh, but she did. Jesse leaned back and took in the fullness of her. "Witness protection huh? So you changed your life, meaning you had a different name."

Catherine couldn't help but smile. She wiped her face with her sleeve and looked at him again. "Jasmine. My name was Jasmine."

"Of all the stuff," he blew out. "I should have guessed that one," he laughed, running a hand through his hair. "Of course your name was Jasmine. And your sisters?" She took a breath.

"Rosemary was Roslyn and M.J. well, she was Sadie, though she doesn't remember any of that now. She was barely five when we moved. She knows we had a life before, that our father died, but not all of it. Rosemary and I never speak of it when she's around."

"And Hannah?"

"Oh she would kill me if I told you that. *Mamm* hated her name, hated it. I might keep that to myself."

For the next few moments they changed topics. Catherine didn't want to linger on the past any more than Jesse did. Telling him the truth surprisingly lifted it from her. Sharing that hurt, the burden with another, made it lighter, easier. They toured the rest of the house-in-progress. Jesse explained the layout he had in mind for four bedrooms and a barn to the southern side of the parcel.

"That's a lot of bedrooms," she remarked, taking another sip of her cola. "I pray you find all the joy in the world here and fill each of them. You really deserve that, Jesse. I hope you know that."

"It's what I want most, a family, but that wouldn't be up to me." He moved, leaning towards her. "That would be up to you." Catherine's breath ceased in his implication. "I was not the best kid. I used to tease girls I thought were *schee* and get into trouble to get their attention. I thought that was the only way to get attention." He brushed her cheek with the backside of his hand. "But I have learned a lot since then."

"Perhaps we have both learned a lot since then." Catherine's heart was thumping wildly in her chest.

"I never had a family like you do. My *daed* would never knock down giants for me," he shrugged. "Things may never be right between him and me, you should know," he swallowed back the regret of it. She did know. Her heart went out to him.

"I admire you for trying so hard, for looking ahead, hoping to create something better." What he wanted most in this life was exactly what she wanted to give him.

"With the right partner, I know I can have the family I have always wanted and an extension to the family you already have." Fresh tears made themselves witness to this moment she knew she would never forget if she lived to be a hundred. "I love you, Catherine Faith Raber. Always have. From the moment you screamed at me for M.J. getting hurt, to that night at the youth gathering you gave Addie your apron, I have loved you."

"You knew about that," she said, earning her a laugh.

"You can't stand to have a hair out of place. Of course I noticed. I've noticed everything. The way you move so lightly, but with purpose. The way you bite your lip," his thumb brushed her bottom lip, "when you are thinking real hard about something." He leaned closer. "I want this future, in this house, with our *kinner*. I've wandered too long, and prayed even longer, for this. I want to build our lives better, give our family everything we missed. And I want to start right now."

She gasped at his declarations. "Me? You want to do all of this with me?"

"I can't, I won't do it without you." Funny thing about tears: the pesky things were just too slippery to keep in place. He leaned into her, kissing the dampness on her cheek. Her insides flipped, fluttered, and warmed as his lips trailed down and paused a breath away from her own.

"Marry me. Build this house with me. Be the *mamm* to our

kinner and the love of my life." His lips teased a light brush and retreated. "Let me kiss you every day for the rest of our lives. Though I will say, Daniel is of the mind we have a long courtship. I'm not"

"Yes," she breathed out. "To both," she wrapped two arms around him.

Catherine's Peach Cobbler

1 jar of canned peaches, drained of syrup.
½ c. butter
1 c. self-rising flour (if using all purpose flour, add 2 tsp baking powder and a ½ tsp salt)
1 c. sugar
1 c. milk

Instructions

Preheat the oven to 350°F. Place the butter in a 10-inch baking dish and set the pan in the warm oven. While the butter is melting, combine the flour and sugar in a medium size bowl and whisk to combine. You may add a dash of cinnamon, but that's optional. Add the milk and whisk smooth. Remove the melted butter from the oven, and rotate the pan to coat the bottom. Using a spoon (so as not to splash hot butter on you) place peaches in butter, then carefully pour the batter in an even layer over the top. Bake at 350°F for 35-45 minutes, until the crust is golden brown.

Here is a sneak peek into book 2 in the Daniel's Daughters series

Saving Daniel's Daughter

Warm morning air wafted through the open doors and windows carrying a mixture of summer, paint, and sawdust through the newly erected house. Paul Eicher adjusted the lamp in his dark corner. Hanging trim in the wee morning hours was strenuous on the eyes, but thirty degrees cooler on the body. Last day of August heat offered no respite for any man in Miller's Creek, Kentucky, especially one helping his dearest friend put the finishing touches on his new home. If Jesse wanted to surprise his bride-to-be with a finished kitchen before daybreak, then Paul would do his part to help. Because that's what friends were for, and Paul liked to think himself a good friend.

Paul liked busy. He lent a hand when needed in his father's leather shop, worked at the Raber sawmill five days a week, and volunteered twice a month with the local fire department. Busy always helped the days pass without being reminded he was twenty-five and alone. Evenings, now that was a whole different matter. Living in a big empty house allowed a man ample hours to ponder over his single status.

Across the room, Jesse painted trim around the kitchen windows an acceptable shade of antique white and hummed like a lovesick schoolboy. Why anyone would paint over wood, Paul could only wonder. It should be varnished, enhancing its beauty, not hid under splatters of overlay. Paul had an eye for potential where few took notice. Driving another finishing nail into the stained wall trim, he felt what he had never felt before. Envy.

Jesse had only returned to Miller's Creek in April after eight years wandering in the world, and now, four months later, was marrying the woman he had loved since he was old enough to know what love was—painting trim instead of varnishing it and humming. It was a tad frustrating. Paul had followed his Amish upbringing to a perfect point and hadn't a thing to hum about.

"You've practically built this house. Sure I can't return the favor for you?" Jesse asked breaking Paul out of his wallowing. The bartering system need not apply to *freinden*, and Jesse couldn't help him with the one thing Paul couldn't manage to do himself. Start a family.

"My house is already built if you haven't noticed," Paul said coolly and stood, stretching out the kink in his back. In another hour his shift at the mill would begin, and another day of normalcy would carry on. Good thing he was blessed with a strong back and a heaping load of patience.

"I noticed," Jesse said shooting him a look. "But its…" Jesse hesitated.

"Empty," Paul quickly finished. His home was two stories tall with three bedrooms, and thanks to a healthy woodworking habit passed down by his *dawdi*, full of more furniture than one house needed.

"Well, empty on the things that matter, but that can be remedied if you weren't so stubborn," Jesse scoffed.

"A confident man and a stubborn one aren't the same," Paul countered and began unhooking his tool belt. "I've tried courting, you know it, but…" Paul groaned.

"Trust," Jesse suggested.

"Says the man who is readying his *haus* for his new bride and lots of *kinner*." Paul shot back not meaning to sound sarcastic. It wasn't in his nature. Between the heat that made a man sweat buckets before getting out of bed and his lonesome mood, Paul was feeling a bit off pudding this particular Monday.

"I grew up an only child with a *daed* who would have

traded me in for a *hund* any day. You had a large family. I'm adding to my life. I'm happy," Jesse said.

"Hummingly so," Paul uttered.

"Get a dog," Jesse said without a hint of humor in it.

"A dog?" The last thing Paul needed was a *hund* to care for. Between working and helping love-struck *freinden*, who had time?

"A man needs a dog." Paul shot him an unimpressed look. "Or, you could try courting again." He could, but Paul wasn't about pretending he could find what he wanted in the available *maedels* of Miller's Creek when his heart knew none of them were her.

Rosemary Raber had been a couple years behind them school, a quiet, shy girl with more dark hair than one *kapp* could contain. They had grown up together practically, Rosemary and her sisters, and Paul and his two closest friends, Jesse and Aiden. They often times found themselves crossing paths over the years, yet never treading the same one. It was reason enough for Paul to accept work at her father's mill, a chance to get to know her better. Which was a hard task to conquer when she seldom left the family farm. Harder, since she refused any man's attention towards her.

"You and I both know courting isn't for me. I just don't have the same charms as you." Paul smirked smugly.

"You have your own charms," Jesse laughed. "I'm sure some poor woman out there might find them appealing."

"But not her."

"She has her reasons, Paul." Jesse cleared his throat. "Rosemary is cautious, and practically runs that whole farm." Jesse waved a hand east. "She takes Edith shopping on Thursdays and that frets her something terrible most days."

Paul had seen her leave plenty on a Thursday to fetch the Bishop's *fraa*. Since Rosemary moved to Miller's Creek, Paul made it a point to know her, and everything about her. Her favorite color was yellow. She loved animals and the outdoors better than people, and baked as well as his *mamm*. Her quiet was often mistaken for shy, but he'd seen her firsthand throw-up a fuss at Aiden Shetler for teaching her youngest sister how to ride a horse backwards when they were *youngies*. He knew everything except whatever Jesse meant by, "she has her reasons for being cautious."

"We talk from time to time. Rosemary is quite the talker once you find something she is interested in talking about." Paul groaned again. His best friend had gotten further with Rosemary in four months than his years. Yeah, sin or not, Paul was envious.

"You're not going to tell me are you?" Paul was there when Jesse needed a friend growing up, the hard childhood he had, and was there again when he returned, helping him find his footing in the community again. Jesse owed him an explanation.

"*Nee*. Not my place. If you want to know more about her, afraid you're going to have ask her." What were friends for? Paul growled.

"Perhaps a dog isn't such a bad idea." Paul made his way to the door just as the waking sun broke over Sugar Hill. "You enjoy the day with Catherine while the rest of us sweat it out at the mill." Jesse and Catherine were spending a working Monday shopping for their new home and running errands while Paul worked under a hot August sun.

"Oh, I will," Jesse called back playfully as Paul slipped out into another day.

By mid-day Paul's gaze began to rifle the fading green hillside and well-worn path leading to the Raber's house next door. At this hour, Hannah should be mounting the hill to come deliver a noon meal. He was famished. It was one of the few perks given working for Daniel Raber. Paul couldn't do more beyond frying eggs or making lumpy pancakes. Weekday day lunches were a blessing.

"Are you really going to the dog pound, yet," Sam Lewis asked as he caught a board off the edger and added it to the stack at his left. Paul pulled his gaze from the hillside and nodded.

"Animal shelter," he corrected. He never understood why people referred to such a place as 'a pound'. Paul had thought about Jesse's idea all morning and though a dog was the last thing he needed, but the idea held some appeal. Aside from the livestock and few barn cats growing up, Paul had never actually owned a dog before. *Daed* always said there wasn't much sense in having a thing that didn't serve a purpose. Right now, a dog's purpose was to distract a man from his dismal future and perhaps keep a few chickens safe from predators.

"My *bruder* Felty has *hunds*," Sam rolled his green blue eyes. "All they do is smell and bark all the time." Sam removed his hat and wiped the sweat from his brow. "Then again, that's what happens when you don't do a thing with them." Sam shook his head.

Paul knew Felty Lewis well enough to know he already pitied any dog leashed to him. The Lewis brothers had a reputation for not tending to their animals and for challenging the rules. It was just a few months ago Sam himself had been caught racing buggies with a scared *maedel* at his side. Unlike Felty, Sam felt horrible about the ordeal and gave a rare Lewis apology for his actions. That's when Paul and Jesse decided to convince Daniel to give the fella a job. With Aiden gone tending to his sick *onkel*'s farm, they were shorthanded as it was. Paul missed his friend, but had to admit Sam Lewis could outwork Aiden any day of the week. Who knew a Lewis had a knack for hard work. It was Sam's negative attitude Paul and Jesse hoped to work on next. Poor Sam was simply a product of being raised by a hardened lot, but Paul saw the potential there, under the bad egg facade. Sam had heart.

"Hiya, Rosemary," Sam greeted. Paul whipped around and sure enough there she was, like a whisper sneaking past him and looking like summer and fall all wrapped into one. At the sight of her, his heart began doing that hard hammering thing it was prone to do anytime she was within range.

Rosemary nodded and made her way to the office porch where lunch was often served. To his left, Daniel shut down the motor on the mill sending the saw blade into the slow winding down screech before resting altogether. No one needed an invitation to eat. Paul removed his work gloves and pocketed them in the back of his trousers and fell into line with Sam, Daniel, and Vernon making their way to the office porch. Trying to recover from his missed opportunity of speaking to her, he quickly caught up to Rosemary.

"Let me help," he offered. Without slowing her stride, Rosemary shot him a confused over her shoulder.

"I've got it." She said facing forward again and made her way up the office steps. Her dainty shoulders slanted by the weight of the full basket and her shoes barely making a smacking noise with every step. Like her father, Rosemary was reserved and focused, a roving eye to her surroundings. She was aware of everything about, and yet, kept herself limited.

Paul studied her more closely. It wasn't a hardship. But after Jesse's remark, he wanted to know what made someone so young, beautiful, and full of life, keep herself closed off. Had someone broken her delicate heart, or was trust something she had difficulty with? He would gladly help remedy whatever kept her eyes staring downward so often.

While Sam inspected his straw hat for weaknesses, Rosemary began pulling plastic containers out of a basket. Daniel retrieved five bottles of water, handing one to each of them, including Rosemary. She gave her father a scrunched look as she peered beyond the office door. No doubt waiting for Catherine to emerge from the office. Rosemary rarely delivered lunch but when she did, usually she and Catherine sat at one end of the porch, chatting.

A hot breeze picked up, flinging a few stray hairs from her face. Her hair was the color of morning *kaffi*, and her eyes always reminded him of *mamm*'s chocolate frosted brownies. His stomach growled hungrily. Only Paul wasn't sure it was food he wanted.

"Where are Catherine and Jesse?" Rosemary asked Daniel who currently had his mouth filled a cookie. Paul gladly spoke up.

"They went to get their marriage license and pick up a few things for their *haus*." Paul answered. Rosemary nodded primly then turned her eyes on her father again.

"That doesn't take all day," she muttered.

"You know Jesse," Paul chuckled. "Getting out of work and spending time with Catherine is his new talent."

"And he's good at it," Daniel laughed. Rosemary didn't seem to find his humor funny, not with her features all scrunched up like that. Paul let out a breath. Talking to women was like pulling good teeth. The chance of one day filling out for one of those licenses was about as good as Sam Lewis over there smiling. Poor fella spent far too much time frowning.

When Daniel stepped away to tend to an arriving customer, Paul decided today he would give it one more shot. If all else failed, there was the animal shelter.

MORE ABOUT MINDY STEELE

More About Mindy Steele

Raised in Kentucky timber country, Steele is a best-selling and award-winning author who writes of her rural surroundings. Winner of the 2022 and 2024 FHL Reader's Choice award, Steele has been a welcomed addition to the Amish genre. Her knowledge and admiration for the Amish credits her ability to understand boundaries, and customs, giving her readers an inside view of the Plain life. Her accidental debut into romantic suspense proves she is a writer of words and a storyteller at heart. Her books are peppered with humor, and sprinkled with grace, charming all the senses to make you laugh, cry, hold your breath, and root for the happy ever after ending.

Steele lives in northeastern Kentucky with her husband, Mike. They have five grown children, eleven grandchildren, and many wonderful neighbors.

Mindy loves connecting with readers. You can connect with her at Mindysteele.com or one of her social pages.

https://www.facebook.com/mindy.h.steele
https://www.instagram.com/msteelem07/
https://www.goodreads.com/author/show/14181261.
Mindy_Steele
https://amazon.com/author/mindysteele